The Family that Lies

Forsaken by Grayce, Saved by Merci

D1517909

The Family that Lies

Forsaken by Grayce, Saved by Merci

Published by Lakisha Johnson
ISBN-13:

978-1539771012

ISBN-10:

1539771016

Dedication

Lakisha dedicates this book to each of you who continually support me. With so many authors out there, you don't have to be supportive of me and when you are; I am grateful. Please don't stop. Your support fuels me.

Laquisha dedicates this book to Velma Jean Fields (my mother in love) who I called "Momma Dear". You accepted me with no questions asked, always treating me as if I was one of yours. You loved me even when I was not even worthy of it and too foolish to accept it. Your words encouraged me, your strength inspired me and your spirit rests in me! I love you with my whole heart because you first loved me and I pray that you will continue to love me in death the same way you loved my in life. Rest in paradise "Momma Dear" until we shall meet again.

Lakisha's Acknowledgements

As always, I have to thank God for His mercies that are new every morning. He is awesome in all His ways!

To my husband, Willie, my children Gabrielle and Christopher and my entire family; know that I love each of you for supporting me. To my twin sister Laquisha, you rocked out on your first book and I am very proud of you. I love you chick!

To my awesome editor, Steph and book cover designer Angel Bearfield of Dynasty Covers ... You ladies rock! Thank you for building lasting relationships and making it so easy to work with you.

To the awesomeness of B.M. Hardin, words will never convey my thankfulness to all you done! You are a black woman who rocks!!

To every one of you who support Lakisha, in every capacity; THANK YOU! I cannot believe this is my tenth book. However, I know I wouldn't be the author I am without supporters like you purchasing, downloading, reading, reviewing and recommending my books.

To those of you who are on this journey or aspiring to write, don't give up. It's hard work but it's worth it. Connect with me on social media.

https://www.facebook.com/AuthorLakisha/

Instagram: KishaJohnson | Twitter: @_kishajohnson

I'd love to hear from you.

Laquisha's Acknowledgements

I'm a simple nobody trying to live in the purpose set out for me so I must thank God for His everlasting grace, mercy, wisdom and knowledge. Without Him I am nothing.

To my mommy lady Fannie Stovall, thank you for always supporting your girls, for making the sacrifices look easy and for loving us. I love you to the moon and back!

To my girls Maria, Marcia and Michaiah, everything I do is to make yours better and I'll go to my grave doing just that because you all deserve nothing less. My love for you is undying and I pray it shows and that you know!

To my sisters: Lakisha (Marcy) girl, I could take up every page of this book telling of your goodness and kindness to me but I will settle for these few lines. There will never, in this lifetime, be enough thanks I could give to repay you for being my keeper when I couldn't keep myself! I love you beyond measure but you knew that already. Essie (my Thang as I call her) thank you for always speaking positive things over my life and for the encouragement and love you give me daily. You bless me and most times do not even know it. Shoney Bee thank you for being the big sister you are. From telling a story that'll make you cry with laughter to keeping the conversation and the block hot!

To my brothers Leon, Katron and Robert, aunts, uncles, nieces, nephews, cousins near and far and my BFFs; thank you for loving me in everything I venture out to do never questioning rhyme or reason, just show up packed for the ride.

The Family that Lies

Forsaken by Grayce, Saved by Merci

Prologue

"Yea," I answer the phone, rolling back over into the bed. "Hello."

"Merci!" my mom screams.

"Yes Mother, what's wrong now?" I reply in my groggy voice.

"It's Grayce," she wails.

"What's Grayce?"

"She, she…" Mom stutters.

"Mom, it's early. Can I call you back when I get up?"

"She, uh, Grayce was attacked."

Springing up in the bed, I scream, "Attacked? Is she ok?"

"I don't know," she cries.

"What do you mean? Where is she?"

"We're at Regional One. The doctors don't know much yet. All they've said is that it doesn't look good. Merci, you need to get here, please!"

"I'm on my way."

I get up and quickly dress, grabbing my bags that I packed last night. I call the airport to see about changing to an earlier flight from New York back home to Memphis. Thank God I am able to get on the 6:30am one. I say a quick prayer for my sister as I rush to check out of the hotel.

After an almost three-hour flight, I finally make it to my car in long-term parking at the airport. Throwing my bags in, I jump into the driver's seat. Doing over 90 mph on the expressway I reach the hospital. I find a parking spot, quickly turn off the car engine and run inside.

"May I help you?" the receptionist asks as I walk into complete chaos.

"Yes ma'am, I'm looking for a patient's room, Grayce Alexander."

"Alexander," she says, tapping on the keyboard with a pace slower than a snail.

"Yes, G-R-A-Y-C-E Alexander."

"Here she is. She's in the trauma bay. Go down to the double doors and I'll buzz you in. Then you will need to go to the nurses' station on your left and they will be able to help further."

Going through the doors, I power walk to the nurses' station. Before I make it, I hear Mom call my name.

Running to her, I ask, "Mom, how is she?"

"It's really bad. They are prepping her for surgery."

"Surgery? No, they can't. Where's the doctor?"

"You just missed him by twenty minutes."

"I'll be back," I say, leaving her standing there.

Getting to the nurses' station, I let the nurse on duty know who I am and I ask her to page the doctor who is handling Grayce's chart. After what seems like forever, he calls back. The nurse hands me the phone.

"This is Dr. Felix."

"Dr. Felix, my name is Merci Alexander. I was told you're the one taking care of my sister Grayce. Can you please tell me what's going on? My mom says you're taking her to surgery but she's pregnant?"

"Yes ma'am, we became aware of her pregnancy when we performed an ultrasound of her abdomen, but right now she's very critical. Your sister suffered some cracked ribs and blunt force trauma to her head. The trauma has caused some bleeding on her brain and surgery is the only option we have to save her life."

"Oh my God. What about the babies?"

"As of now, they are stable and haven't been affected by Ms. Alexander's trauma. There's no sign of oxygen deprivation but I won't lie to you. This isn't going to be easy. I will do my best to save your sister but I have to ask, if it comes down to choosing between your sister and the babies—"

"Save my sister."

"Very well. It is my hope to save them all but I won't make you a promise I can't keep. Now, I have to go. The nurses will keep you updated throughout the surgery and I will be out to speak to you as soon as we're done."

"Thank you, doctor."

Walking back to where my parents are, I remember to call Thomas. With everything going on, I hadn't even thought about it until now.

He answers, still half asleep. "Babe, is everything alright? I thought your flight wasn't until later."

"Thomas, Grayce is hurt. She's at Regional One being prepped for surgery."

"I can be there in a few minutes. What time is your flight?"

"I'm already home, I took an earlier flight when my mom called. I've been here about fifteen minutes," I say trying to hold back my tears.

"Ok, I'm on the way."

Hanging up, I see Mom is standing there.

"Merci, what did the doctor say?"

"They're taking her to surgery. He said the nurses will keep us updated."

"That's it? Is she awake? Is she talking? What?"

"Mom, calm down. He didn't say any of that. All he said is that she needs surgery as soon as possible."

"I knew we shouldn't have left her."

"Left her where?"

"At your house."

"Are you kidding me, right now? Of all things to say, you picked this? I didn't make Grayce stay with me, she chose to. Furthermore, what does my house have to do with any of this?"

"That's where she was attacked."

"What? By who?"

"I don't know."

"Well, what are the police saying?"

"Nothing yet."

"You're not making sense, Mother, what happened?" I ask, getting agitated.

"I don't have all the details. Apparently Grayce dialed 911 while she was being attacked. They were able to trace the call to your address but by the time they got there, whoever did this was gone. They left my baby sprawled on the living room floor covered in blood. They left her there to die."

"This is crazy. How would someone get in without the alarm going off?"

"I don't know."

"Well, how did you all find out?"

"One of the officers at the scene is a member of the church. He called us once he recognized her. Merci, I just don't understand why this would happen to her. Grayce would never hurt anyone. Who would do something like this to her?"

"I did," a voice says from behind us.

Turning around, my Mom's eyes open wide in shock.

"You? Why would you hurt my baby?" Mom screams.

The woman standing there calmly states, "Because she was fucking my husband!"

Merci

"Ugh," I moan as we pull up to my house.

"What's wrong?"

"My parents are here."

"Does that mean I can't come in for a night cap?"

"That's exactly what it means, but thank you for a lovely dinner, Justice," I say, leaning over to give him a kiss once he places the truck in park.

"Um," he says, wiping his mouth. "You need to stop before you wake the monster."

"Looks to me like it's too late," I say, rubbing between his legs.

"You have that effect on him."

"Good to know," I smile while unzipping his pants, freeing him from his boxers.

"What are you doing?" he says, looking around.

"Giving you that night cap."

"With your parents in the— Oh shit!"

I savor his taste while slowly taking him inch by inch into my mouth.

"Damn!" he says, grabbing the back of my head as I take all of him in, causing saliva to drop from my mouth.

"Just like that, ugh, like that! Shit!"

I begin sucking harder and faster.

He has both hands on my head as I relax my jaws to allow all of him in. I move up, releasing him before wiping the corners of my mouth.

"Wait," he says, realizing I've stopped. "I know you aren't going to leave me like this?"

"Why not? Can't you handle the rest by yourself?"

"Hell no! Come on baby, don't do me like this. Have mercy on me."

I laugh before taking him back between my lips.

"Yes baby, suck that—"

Just then there is a knock on the window.

"Merci, what in the hell are you doing?" my sister asks while looking around.

I hit the button, letting the window down. "This is a penis, Grayce, and what I'm doing is called giving head. You want to try it?"

"Our parents are right in the house and you're out here in the driveway doing this nasty stuff. What if Dad had been the one to come out?"

"He would have seen the same thing you did. Now, go back in the house, he's coming. I mean, I'm coming." I laugh as I hit the automatic button to let the window back up.

Resuming my position, I tighten my jaw muscles, slurping and sucking while increasing my pace until I feel his release going down my throat.

"Damn girl!" he says, breathing hard. "What a hell of a night cap."

"Thank you again for a lovely night."

Getting out of the truck, I wipe my mouth, fix my hair and run my hand down my dress.

I let out a loud sigh before pushing open the door of the house. Placing my purse on the table, I walk into the den with all eyes on me.

"What's up, parents? What are you guys doing here, again?" I say, bothered by their presence.

"Where have you been?" my dad barks.

"Handling grown folk business," I reply, rolling my eyes.

"Girl, don't you sass me," Dad says.

"Yep, that's my cue to leave. It was good seeing the both of you. Let's do this again, um … never," I say as I head towards my room.

"Merci Renee Alexander, don't you dare walk away from us."

"Mom, every time you guys come here, it's with the intention to start an argument with me. Well, not tonight. I'm tired but, more importantly, I'm grown and I stopped having to explain myself to either of you at the age of seventeen."

"Why can't you be respectful like your sister?" Dad yells.

"Because I am not my sister," I yell back. "And I am sick of being compared to her. She's who she is and I am who I am."

"Dad, please stop," Grayce screams. "Why do you always do this? We are not children anymore!"

"You could have fooled me," he says, "Ever since you were a teenager, Merci, you've been the one to give us the most trouble. I just don't understand for the life of me why Grayce would want to live here with you."

I laugh as he continues.

"You out there in that truck doing God knows what with God knows who while we are right here in the house. You need to get your life together, little girl, because God isn't going to keep sparing you."

"Sparing me from what, Daddy? You?"

"Keep acting like this is a joke."

"Oh no, the only joke here is you because while you play dress up in your pastoral robe, you need to know that God isn't going to keep sparing you either."

"What is that supposed to mean?" he asks.

"Figure it out. I'm going to bed. Grayce, be sure to lock up after they leave."

"Merci," my mom yells. "Why do you always run instead of handling things like an adult?"

"Are you serious? What I am doing right now is walking away from the both of you before I say something I shouldn't.'"

"No! You are running just like you did when you were seventeen."

"You call it running, I call it saving my own life because apparently you didn't give a damn about the way your husband treated me."

"You can call it whatever you want but we can all see what a mistake that was to let you leave," Dad bellows.

"You didn't let me do anything. I left because I had to and just so you know, *Daddy*, the only mistake I made was allowing Grayce to move into my house. Had I known it came with you and her, I would have slammed the door in her face."

"Is that what Christians do to family?" my dad laughs.

"Oh you can find that funny but do Christians beat the crap out of their child like you did to me? You know what, screw this. You will not stand within the walls of my house and treat me like you did when I was in yours. If you can't respect me, there's the door." I turn to leave but I change my mind. "Oh, another thing, you will stop comparing me to Grayce: I am not her. And for the record, I wasn't the one getting into trouble as a teenager; it was just easier for you to blame me rather than your angel Grayce."

"We didn't blame anything on you that you didn't do. You were the one that kept having boys climbing in through your window, not Grayce," he yells.

"Stop lying! All these years and you're still keeping up with that same tired lie. It's cool because karma is a bit—"

"Merci!" Mom yells.

"This is my house. If you don't like what I say and how I say it, you can leave out the same way you came in."

"That's enough!" my sister screams.

"Is it?" I yell, turning to face her. "Is it enough, Grayce? Is it enough that I'm being consistently blamed for your mistakes? Why don't you tell him? Go on, Grayce, tell dear Daddy your secrets."

Grayce

"What secrets? What is she talking about, Grayce?"

"I don't know. Can we please just drop this?" I say as tears begin to fall.

"Look what you've done. Now you've made your sister cry," Dad says walking towards me. "Merci, you are evil and I will not allow my daughter to live under your roof another night."

"Oh please, those aren't real tears. However, if you're ready to pack her stuff, I have some boxes in the garage. Shall I get them, sister?"

"Stop! It's too much to deal with," I tell them.

"Oh, this is too much to deal with? Yea, ok. All three of you are a bunch of liars and you're right, Dad, Grayce doesn't need to be influenced by me. So how about we do this: you can come by in the morning and get her and her shit. Does that work for yawl?"

"Merci, please talk to me," my mom pleads. "We are just worried about you, that's all."

She holds up her hand to stop her. "Save it, Mother. You aren't worried about me, but it did sound good though. You know, I cannot for the life of me understand how I managed to survive in a house full of liars. Liars for parents and a liar for a sister — all of you are nothing more than a band of evil. And yet you've made me out to be the black sheep of the family when I've never earned the title. I'm just glad I got out when I did. And so the both of you know, I have no plans to be like Grayce. She's the one stuck to daddy's coat tail, not me. I have my own identity and it's too bad you all can't see it."

My mom is standing with her mouth open.

"What happened to you?" Mom asks as tears start to flow.

"I started thinking for myself?"

I let out a huge sigh as Merci storms out. My dad starts in again. "Baby girl, why do you continually put up with your sister's mess? Why don't you just move back with us until you can find a place of your own?"

"Daddy, you know I can't do that."

"Why not?"

"Because I am grown. How would it look for me to still be at home with my parents? Living here with Merci isn't all that bad. She doesn't get like this until you all show up with this foolishness. I've asked you both to stop comparing us and if you can't, you may need to stop coming around when she's here."

"I just don't understand that girl. She has her whole life in front of her yet she chooses to live like a harlot. I'm sorry Grayce, but I won't sit by and watch her destroy your life in the process of destroying hers. We've worked too hard to give you a great life."

"Yes, but it isn't your choice on how we live, Daddy. We are both adults and have to make our own decisions. I know you want what's best but this, the arguing, this isn't it. You are only making things worse. The bible says in Proverbs 22:6—"

"I know what it says, Grayce, but—"

"There is no 'but' because this is getting out of hand. Each time you two come here it's getting worse and worse. What do you think you're solving? The more you push at her, the more she's going to push back."

"We know this, Grayce, but we all know your sister isn't making the right choices these days."

"How do you know what choices she's making? You all never take the time to find out about her life; you automatically assume you know when you don't."

"What else are we supposed to do? She made the choice not to have us in her life. If it wasn't for you moving here, we would never see her."

"Can you blame her? I wouldn't want to see you all either if this is what I had to look forward to."

"Why are you taking up for her?" Mom asks.

"I'm not but it's the truth. When Merci left at seventeen, did either of you try to fix the relationship with her? Did either of you resolve the issue of the real reason why she left?"

"No, she made the decision to leave; we didn't make her."

"She was a child, Mother. You know what, forget it. I don't want to argue anymore. I'm tired and I have some papers to grade."

"We're sorry, Grayce. We didn't mean to come here tonight to argue. We hadn't seen you since Sunday and wanted to make sure you were alright."

"That's fine but until this mess dies down between you all, call before you come."

"Fine. Are we still on for lunch after church on Sunday?"

"Yes."

"Good. Maybe you can talk Merci into coming," Mom says.

"I don't know, what for?" Dad says.

"See, that's what I'm talking about. Goodnight Daddy."

"Grayce, we love you and we're sorry for everything tonight. We love you," Mom says, giving me a hug.

"I love you too."

Merci

After making it to my room, I slam the door. I didn't have to but I wanted to make sure they heard it. Ugh, they get on my freaking nerves. Always showing up at my damn house trying to tell me what I need to do. I am twenty-nine years old with no children, a great job and I pay my own bills. I don't need them telling me how to run my life. I've been doing a good job by myself.

We used to have a great life, the four of us, but when I turned fourteen something changed. I don't know what it was or why it happened but all I know is, I woke up one morning and my life was suddenly different.

Grayce and I are seventeen months apart, and for as long as I can remember we were both 'daddy's girls' but then he started treating me like I had a contagious disease or that I'd killed his cat. He started acting differently towards me, treating me like he hated me. Then it was, "You need to be more like your sister," "You're nothing but a whore," "You're evil." My dad was so hateful to me but then he'd stand in the pulpit on Sunday morning declaring that you've got to love your brothers and sisters. What a crock of shit!

I mean, how can you preach one thing and live another? I don't know the answer to that but what I do know is I'm sick of it. I live my life on my terms. I don't ask them for anything and damn sure don't need them. I've been on my own since I was seventeen, and if I can survive that, I can survive anything.

Anyway, enough of that. Let me introduce myself. My name is Merci Renee Alexander and you've probably already figured out that Grayce and I are sisters. Although we were born seventeen months apart, we can pass as twins. But according to our parents, she's the good daughter and I am the spawn of Satan.

Our dad, Melvin Alexander, is the founder and senior pastor of Emmanuel Grace Church and my mom, Gina, takes her role as First Lady way too seriously.

As for me, I've been a Senior Account Executive at Glassor Finance for over ten years. Grayce is an elementary school teacher who is dating the associate pastor's son, Shaun, and me, well, according to dad, I'm dating the entire city of Memphis. Grayce goes to church three times a week, and although my dad thinks I'm a heathen, I attend church on Sundays.

Yes, I was raised in the church but when I took the blinders off, I finally saw that all the so-called saints at Emmanuel, who are shouting on Sunday, are just hypocrites who still sin Monday through Saturday. This is why I will not go back to my dad's church under any circumstance.

Speaking of my dad, he is no saint himself. He can continue to fool his congregation with that tired holy and sanctified façade, but I know him and he's nothing but a lying sinner, just like the folk who hang on his every word Sunday after Sunday.

That's why I mind my own business but they just won't let me be great! I don't go to his house telling him how to run his life so I'll be damned if I let him come here and tell me how to run mine. I don't give him advice and I don't need his. I'm living on my terms only and if I go to heaven or hell, it'll be nobody's fault but mine.

God and I have our own personal relationship and although I am not perfect, He knows my heart.

Grayce

After showing Mom and Dad out and locking the door, I sit down on the couch replaying what just happened. Sadly, it's a scene that we've seen far too many times lately.

Every time our parents stop by it's the same thing. They yell then Merci yells and nothing gets resolved. Yes, I understand her position and I get theirs too; they are our parents but being sisters always leaves me caught in the middle.

They still treat me like I'm a child; that's why I left their house eight months ago. I couldn't take living under their thumb anymore. They want to know everything I do and who I do it with. No, I am not perfect but Dad seems to think so.

I don't know what made me come to Merci for help but I did. Our relationship had really been non-existent since she left the house twelve years ago, and I can't blame her. I thought she would shut the door in my face, but instead she let me in.

I cried and begged her to let me stay and she did. I don't think I could be that forgiving but she was. Now, I'm hoping to rebuild our relationship. I might be able to, if I could just get our parents off her back before she kicks me out on the street. I have to fix this because God knows I love my parents but I cannot move back with them.

Yes, Merci has her faults but who doesn't. Growing up, she never argued or fought but lately that's all she does and it's becoming too much. I plan on talking to Mom and Dad about this at lunch on Sunday because something has got to give.

Shaking my head, I head down the hall to Merci's room and knock.

"What?" she screams.

"It's me," I say opening the door. "You want to get some dinner?"

"No, leave me alone, Grayce. I'm not in the mood for your theatrics tonight."

"Dang it Merci, I only came to see if you wanted something to eat. You don't have to bite my head off. Besides, you know they only want the best for you," I say, sitting on the bed.

"Since when? Grayce, come on now, you know their best for me is to be more like you. Well, news flash, I am not you. I am not the perfect daughter of the Alexanders and, if I'm being honest, neither are you."

"I never said I was perfect."

"Oh, I know you're not."

"What is that supposed to mean?"

"Girl, please! You may be playing your mom and dad but you aren't playing me. While you're walking around acting like you're the perfect preacher's kid, I know for a fact if I were to open the door to your closet, some skeletons will fall out."

"Look, don't blame me for what our parents say and do. I never portrayed myself as the flawless child and I've never asked for you to be compared to me. The same way you don't apologize for the way you live, I won't apologize for the way I live."

"I didn't say you had to apologize but stop acting like you have it all together. When Mom and Dad come around you go into this shell of a thirteen-year-old girl who doesn't have a tongue to speak for herself. They can dictate to you what you should be doing, how you should be dressing, who you should be dating and where you worship and you eat it up without a second thought. You are a puppet for them and I surely hope one of these days you wake up and cut the strings."

"That's not fair, Cee, and you know it."

I laugh. "You know I'm right because the only time you call me Cee is when I hit a nerve."

"I am not a puppet."

"Who are you trying to convince, Grayce?"

"Can we drop this?"

"You came in my room."

"I only came to see if you wanted to eat. I was in the middle of fixing some pasta when Mom and Dad showed up."

"No, I'm good but thanks."

"Ok," I say getting ready to close her door.

"Oh, and tell your parents to call before they come the next time."

Leaving out of her room, I go into the kitchen to finish the pasta when the doorbell rings.

Opening the door, this dude grabs me and kisses me like he was just released from prison.

My sister clears her throat which causes him to release me.

"How does my sister taste?" she asks him, smiling.

He steps back and looks from me to her while I stand there with my hand over my mouth.

"Justice, this is my sister, Grayce. Grayce, this is Justice."

"Oh shit! You all look like twins."

"You didn't see her tonight at the truck?"

"Um, I was a little preoccupied, remember?"

Merci

Grayce bolts for the kitchen with her mouth covered and her face flustered.

"Babe, I am so sorry. I honestly thought it was you at the door."

"No problem, we're always getting mixed up. What are you doing here?"

"Did you think you were going to leave me hanging tonight?"

"Um, the last I checked, I was the one that was left hanging. You got yours, remember?"

"Well, I am here to give you yours."

I grab his hand and lead him to my bedroom. Closing the door, I push him on the bed as I work to unfasten his pants. I only have a t-shirt on which I quickly remove.

He strips off his shirt and is preparing to take his pants off when he asks, "Are you ready to ride this wave?"

"Not without a life jacket," I say reaching into my nightstand drawer.

"You don't need that," he says, pushing my hand away.

"A lie! You may not need it but I sure do."

"Come on baby. This is our first time, let me feel it raw," he says, trying to kiss me.

"Uh, hell no."

"Girl, stop playing and let me give you what you've been wanting."

"Uh, boy bye," I say, moving away from him and putting my t-shirt back on.

"What?"

"You heard me. Don't worry about taking your pants off."

"Don't be like that, I'm sorry. Come back to bed. I'll make it worth your while."

"No thanks. Put your shirt back on, it's time for you to roll."

He laughs as he grabs his shirt from the floor. "I should have known you'd be a stuck up bitch. Trying to act all snobbish now but you weren't saying that a few hours ago when my dick was down your throat, raw."

"You're absolutely right and I was foolish for doing that, but the fact still remains, I am not having sex with you or anybody else without a condom. Now, I'll be whatever kind of bitch you want, as long as you say it walking out my house. Let me show you out."

Leaving the room with him behind me, I hear Grayce in the kitchen. I open the door and give him time to cross the threshold.

"Oh boo-boo, for the record," I say as he turns around, "Your dick isn't even long enough to reach down my throat. You have a good night now."

I lock the door and set the alarm.

"Your night over already?" Grayce asks when I walk into the kitchen.

"Hell, yes. That fool thought I was going to sleep with him without a condom."

"Didn't you just meet him?"

"Yea, about a month ago but that's not the point. I'm not having sex without a condom."

"But you'll suck on it without a condom."

"Sometimes, but that's different."

"No it's not. You can get the same disease in your mouth as you can down there."

"Whatever, Saint Josephine. What are you cooking?"

"Don't try to change the subject. What are you doing?"

"I'm picking the tomatoes out of your salad."

"Stop," she says, slapping my hand. "Wash your hands, nasty. And you know what I mean. What are you doing with your life? Why are you sleeping with all these random dudes, Cee?"

"Let me ask you a question, Dr. Phil. What random dudes are you referring to? From my calculations, you've only met one and that was tonight. So tell me how you could possibly know I sleep with every guy I go out with?"

"Because—" she says before stopping.

"Say it!"

"Because it's the way you carry yourself."

I laugh. "You are your father's daughter."

"Merci, please stop playing the victim. You live a fancy free life and then get mad when people call you out on it. You're the one with a new boo on your arm every month so you can't get mad if I call you a hoe. Like I say, it's how you carry yourself."

"Oh okay, let me make sure I get what you're saying. So, because I date more than one man I'm a hoe, and because you go to church three days a week you're holy? That's like saying because I have tattoos I'm a sinner, and because you don't you're a saint?"

"That's not what I'm saying."

"Then what are you saying, sister 'know it all', 'got it all figured out', 'I can't do any wrong'? What exactly are you saying?"

"I don't want to argue with you, Cee."

"We're not arguing. This is two sisters having a conversation. Come on, say what you feel? Don't stop now."

She sighs, "I'm just saying, you portray the life of a hoe with the sleeping around and the way you dress but you get offended when someone calls you one. You keep getting all those tattoos and then you get your feelings hurt when someone calls you ghetto. Let's be real."

"So what you're saying is I need to be more like you and hide it better? Oh ok, I'm catching on. What I should do is walk around with dresses down to my ankles because then people will think I'm saving myself for marriage. I should go to church every time the doors open because then people will believe me when I say I'm a saint of God. I should carry myself just like you. Is that about right?"

She doesn't say anything so I continue. "No answer? That's alright, I'll continue. See, baby sister, I will not walk around being a fake because it appeases everyone else. Yes, I have tattoos but they don't make me ghetto because I can go from the street to the board room the same way you can go from saint to sinner. I can carry a conversation with anybody from the dope dealer on the corner to the president of the company. I got it like that. However, don't think for one second that I am fooled by you because while you're trying to act all saved and sanctified, I know the real you."

"What does that mean? This is the real me and I'm not hiding anything."

"Girl bye! You want to be real then let's be real, shall we? You may carry a bible under your arm but you have a freak card in your wallet. You may not dress like a hoe but you have thot like tendencies. While you may have the skirt down to the floor I can bet you don't have underwear on underneath. And this little sham of a relationship of yours, I know it's for show because Shaun is as gay as they come. So while you're being real with me you may want to be real with your damn self."

"Shaun is not gay!" she screams.

"But you didn't deny anything else," I laugh while walking out. "Bye Felecia!"

Grayce

Fuck her! I mumble under my breath as I finish putting the salad and pasta into the refrigerator. I'm not even hungry anymore. She has me so mad acting like she knows me. *She doesn't know me!* I silently scream in my head.

I walk into my bedroom and slam the door as I pace. I don't even know why I came to live with her! Flopping down on the bed, my cell phone rings. I rush to get it from the night stand.

"Hey," I answer.

"Hey. What are you doing?"

"Nothing, Merci just pissed me off."

"About what?"

"Nothing, it's not important, but we need to talk?"

"Ok, is everything alright?"

"No, where are you?"

"I can be at your house in twenty minutes."

"No, I'll come to you."

"OK, well, I'm at home."

I hang up the call and head down the stairs, grabbing my purse before hurrying out the door.

Pulling up to his house, I get out. I reach the front door and it's already open.

"Babe, what's wrong? Why are you so upset?"

"My sister! Man, she knows how to push my buttons."

"Grayce, calm down. What happened?"

"My parents happened. Every time they show up, Merci and I always end up arguing afterwards."

"That's nothing new. It's been that way since you moved over there. You should have moved in with me instead."

"You know my dad wasn't going for that."

"The last time I checked you are good and grown."

"I don't want to argue with you too. Not tonight."

"I'm not trying to argue. What else happened because the many times I've seen you all argue, it has never made you this upset?"

"She knows."

"She who and knows what?"

"My sister, and she knows that you're gay, Shaun."

"How could she possibly know that? Did you tell her?"

"Hell no, you know I would never tell her anything like that."

"How does she know then?" he yells.

"Stop yelling. I told you I don't know."

"Then how can you be sure?"

"It was the way she said it this time. She said that our relationship was a sham because you are as gay as they come."

He laughs.

"I'm glad you can find this funny."

"Girl, calm down and come get a glass of wine."

"Did you not hear what I said? If she starts saying this type of shit in public, people are going to start speculating. I don't need this right now."

"I heard what you said but I'm kind of glad she said something."

"What? Why would you say that?"

"Grayce, how much longer do you think we'll be able to hide this farce of a relationship? It's been almost a year now and I'm tired. I only agreed to do this as a favor to you but—"

"But what, Shaun? It was not only a favor to me but it was to help you too. You are being compensated well for playing this role so don't start crying now."

"All I'm saying is, I am tired of it. I can't live my life like this anymore." He hands me the glass.

"Oh, so you think being an openly gay son of a pastor will sit well with the congregation at Emmanuel? Do you honestly think they will accept you after you come out? Baby, this is as much for you as it is for me."

"Well, I don't care anymore. And in a few weeks, you or Emmanuel Church will no longer be my problem."

"What do you mean?"

"I'm leaving Memphis and moving to New Orleans."

"What in the hell? When?"

"In two months. That's why I was glad when you said we needed to talk. I've been wanting to tell you but didn't know how."

"Just freaking great."

"Look, I know this is a shock to you but I've had my relationship on hold all this time and I can't do it anymore."

"What am I supposed to do, Shaun? You know how my folks are!"

"What you can do is grow the hell up. You act like you're sleeping with your daddy. Are you twenty-eight or eight?"

"Forget this!"

"We can forget it for now but you only have two months to come up with a plan. You can say I broke your heart or whatever, it doesn't matter to me."

I slam the glass into the floor and walk out. Sitting in my truck, I begin to beat on the steering wheel. *Damn! Damn!* What am I going to do now? How am I supposed to keep my father off my back about getting married without Shaun?

I unlock my glove compartment and pull out the other cell phone I have hidden there. I scroll to the number and press call.

"I need to see you. Yea. Ok, I'll meet you there in fifteen."

In less than ten minutes I am pulling into the garage of the condo he keeps. I leave my purse and phone inside the truck and get out.

"Long day?" he asks, pushing the button to let the garage door down.

"Yes, one you wouldn't believe."

"I have just the thing you need," he says, leading me towards the bedroom. "The water is already on for your shower."

I take a quick shower before oiling myself down. I love a man who pays attention to my likes and needs. He makes sure everything I need is here every time I come.

"Damn, you smell good," he smiles, pulling me into him.

"I know, right. This new oil you got smells great."

"The lady at the shop told me you'd love it."

"Did she now?"

"Yes, and judging by the way your skin smells and feels, I take it you do?"

"I'll like it even more if you lick it off of me."

Sitting down on the bed, I slide to the middle and make myself comfortable with the pillows. As he removes his silk pajama pants, I watch anxiously as he crawls towards me. Rubbing his hands up my legs, he pushes them apart as he admires the strip of curly hair I always leave for him, down there.

He doesn't hesitate to take her into his mouth.

"Awl, you feel so good," I say grinding my hips into his tongue.

He continues to feast on the sweetness of my clit until I am screaming his name. Grabbing his head with both hands, I pull him up to me, taking the time to savor my juices on his lips.

"You're so wet, baby," he whispers in my ear before taking it into his mouth while I insert him into me. Spreading my legs, I grab his ass to push him deeper.

"Oh God," I scream out. "Don't stop!"

"Open your eyes," he commands. "I want you to watch me while I make you cum."

"Oh shit!" I scream out, trying to keep my eyes on him but I can't. I bite down on my lip as he stops. He begins thrusting his hips slowly.

"Hmm," is all I manage to say because the words are caught in my throat.

"This pussy is so good," he says, slipping his tongue into my mouth.

I suck his tongue like it's water and I'm lost in the desert. He is sending waves through my body as he slowly pumps into me. He moans into my mouth. He then sits up, raises my legs over his shoulders and increases his pace.

"Aw," he grunts a few times before collapsing beside me. "Damn, girl. You got some good stuff. When are you going to stop playing and be with only me?"

"Don't start that again. You know I have a lot going on right now and the last I checked you were married."

"That is not an issue."

"Why are you killing the mood?" I ask, getting mad.

"I am not killing the mood. I asked a simple question. I'm tired of sharing you. You should be waking up next to me every morning."

"You know I can't do that right now. My father would kill me."

"Grayce, you're a grown ass woman but when it comes to your dad you act as if you cannot make a decision on your own. How much longer do you think this can go on?"

"Apparently not much longer because Shaun is leaving in two months."

He smiles.

"Great! My whole world is about to be blown to pieces and you're smiling."

"Yes, because I'm glad Shaun is leaving. Maybe now it's time you get from under your dad's thumb."

"I am not under my dad's thumb. Just because I don't stir the pot, it doesn't mean there's nothing boiling."

"Wow, you're even beginning to sound like him. Look babe, I love you but I will not continue to be some pawn in this game you're playing with your dad. Why can't we be together?"

"Maybe it's because you're my dad's best friend, Warren, and the fact that you're married. Oh, and that you're old enough to be my dad. Do you honestly think he'll be alright with this relationship?"

"It's not about him and we haven't been best friends in over fifteen years, you know that."

"Yea, but it doesn't change the fact that we can't be together. I like what we have, don't rock the boat."

"Don't rock the boat? Am I only good for sex and that's it?"

"Isn't that all you wanted in the beginning?"

"Yes, but not anymore. I want you, Grayce."

"Well, we both know that can't happen so drop it."

"One of these days you're going to wish you had me."

"Not if my dad finds out. What happened between the two of you anyway? One minute you were the best of friends and then you weren't."

"It's a long story that I don't want to get into."

"That further proves my point. My dad would never go for this relationship and neither will your wife. Anyway, I have to go. I'll talk to you later."

Walking into the house, I try to be as quiet as I can. Setting the alarm I start towards the stairs.

"Walk of shame, huh?"

"Shut up, Merci, I just went for a drive."

"Or was it more like a ride?" She laughs as I head to my room and slam the door.

Merci

"Well, look who decided to grace me with her presence. Long night?"

"No! As a matter of fact I've been up. I was doing my morning devotion and prayer."

"Yea right," I laugh.

"Merci, please don't start with me this morning."

"What am I starting, Grayce? It's funny that you can dish shit out but you can't take it."

"Don't curse at me, and I am not dishing anything out. You're just mad that I don't uphold you in your wrong."

"Girl, I don't need you to uphold me in anything. You fake ass Christians make me sick. You sit up and judge people when most of your lives are far worse. If the truth shall be told, it's going to be a lot more of you fake, saved folks busting the doors of hell open than anybody else. And you know why?"

"No, but I'm sure you're going to tell me."

"It's because people like me aren't walking around under the pretense of being saved in front of people and then acting unsaved behind closed doors. We don't have to because God accepts us flaws and all. But you, 'oh holy one', you walk around hiding more than a fat woman in a spanx."

"I am not about to do this with you. Not today."

"It's cool because I'll tell you the same thing tomorrow."

"Whatever, Merci."

I laugh as she prepares to leave out.

"Oh, speaking of tomorrow, Mom told me to ask if you wanted to join us for lunch. I don't know why but I told her I would," says Grayce.

"Lunch with whom?"

"You know who: Mom, Dad and Shaun."

"Nope, not going to be able to do it."

"Come on, Merci. Maybe we can have an argument free lunch."

"With your Dad there's never an argument free anything so I'll pass this time, and the next."

"Can you at least do it for me?"

"You? Didn't we just finish arguing like five seconds ago?"

"Yea, but Mom wants you there."

"I'll think about it but I am not making any promises."

"Think hard. Owen Brennan about 1:30. Oh, while you're thinking about lunch, why not think about coming to church?"

"Now you're really pushing it."

"It's just church."

"No, it just your dad's church and I ain't going!"

"It's not Dad's church, Merci, its God's."

"Does your daddy know that?"

"I'm done with this conversation. Talking to you is like talking to a wall."

Lunch with the parents

"Hello good people," I say walking up to the table.

"Merci, I am so glad you decided to join us," Mom says.

"You don't have a jacket to cover all that stuff on your arms?" my dad asks before I can even sit down.

"See, this is why I don't come to these little luncheons. You all enjoy."

"Merci, don't leave," my mom says. "Please, stay."

"Not if Dad is going to act like this the entire afternoon. I don't need to be preached to by him."

"Someone needs to preach to you since you aren't in church."

I take a seat across from Grayce. "What makes you think I'm not in church, Father? Just because I don't set foot in that place you call a church, it doesn't mean I don't belong to a place of worship."

"I don't know anyone who would allow you to come to church dressed like that."

"No one allows me to do anything, I do what I want. And, for your information, the place of worship I attend doesn't punish me for my faults and flaws like you and your minions."

"Will you two please stop?" Grayce shouts.

"I didn't start this, your dad did."

Dad rolls his eyes as I grab a menu.

After the waitress takes our order, and *of course I order a mimosa*, I remove my shades to look at Grayce and Shaun, who seem nervous.

"What's up with you two?" I ask.

"What do you mean?"

"You look like you're about to piss your pants at any moment. Ooo, you're pregnant?"

My dad spits his water out.

"No, I'm not pregnant. What are you talking about?"

"I'm just saying you're looking a little suspect right now."

"Merci, can you drop it, please?" Shaun asks.

"Drop what? I asked a question," I reply as the waitress brings my drink.

"Grayce, are you alright? You're not sick are you?" my mom asks rubbing her arm.

"Mom, I'm fine, but since Merci won't leave me the hell alone, I may as well tell you all." She takes a deep breath. "Shaun is leaving."

"What do you mean, leaving?"

"He's been offered a job in New Orleans."

"Oh Shaun, that's great news," my mom beams.

"But what's the catch?" I ask. "If it's only a job, why are you two acting like you just got caught screwing in the balcony of the church. What else is going on?"

She starts stuttering before finally saying, "We've decided to end our relationship which means I'm not going to move with him."

"What do you mean?" Dad asks, getting a little loud. "What happened? Shaun, what did you do to my daughter?"

"Pastor Alexander, with all due respect I haven't done anything to your daughter. We've talked about it and feel this is the best decision for both of us. Grayce doesn't want to move and I am not turning this opportunity down."

"And that's it?" I ask, smiling.

"Dammit, Merci! Leave your sister alone."

"Dad, did you just curse at me?"

Just then the waitress begins delivering the food.

"Look, can we enjoy lunch and talk about this later?" my sister asks looking at me. I tip my glass and smile.

"So Merci, where is this church you're attending?"

"On the other side of the city?"

"Who's the pastor?"

"None of your business."

"Merci!"

"What? I don't need him calling my pastor, inquiring about me. I go to worship, I pay my tithes and I am happy there. He's not about to ruin it."

"I'll find out like I find out everything else," he gripes.

"Well, good luck with that."

I hurry, finish my food and leave. I've had enough of this crowd to last me a lifetime.

Grayce

"That was some lunch," Shaun remarks when we make it to his car.

"Yea, you can say that again."

"Why didn't you tell me about this lie you came up with?"

"I couldn't think of anything else to say. Merci was badgering the crap out of me."

"So what am I supposed to do now? You know there's not a job offer in New Orleans."

"It doesn't matter. I have two months to figure everything out. That fucking Merci gets on my nerves!"

"Calm down, I'm sure we'll work it out."

"Can you drop me off at my car?"

"I thought we were going to catch a movie."

"I don't feel like it anymore."

"I'm sorry, I know this isn't how you wanted things to go but I cannot continue to live like this."

"You're right, this isn't how I wanted things to go but I knew the day would eventually come. Hell, my parents have been pushing us to get engaged since you and your family showed up at the church. And I knew, eventually, we'd have to deal with it. I mean, how much longer could we have kept up this charade without anyone else getting suspicious? I thought I'd be able to end it on my terms, though. That meddling Merci, ugh!"

"What is the deal with her and your parents anyway?"

"They've been at odds since I was thirteen so your guess is as good as mine. I do know that it's only getting worse and I'm tired of being caught in the middle. Now that we're broken up, I need to think of finding a place of my own."

"You'll figure it out," he says before pulling up to the church. Parking next to my car, one of the three left on the lot, he reaches over and kisses me on the cheek.

"You'll be alright. Call me if you need me."

"Thanks. I will."

"Are you sure you don't want to hang out or something?"

"I'm sure. We'll talk later, I promise."

Getting into my truck, I throw my purse into the passenger seat.

"Shit! Shit!" I scream out to the silence.

Just then someone blows a car horn. I look up to see Mrs. Blair, Shaun's mother. I push the start button and let the window down.

"Are you alright, dear? Where's Shaun?"

"Yes, everything is fine. He just dropped me off after lunch with my parents. What are you still doing here?"

"Darrick and I had some things to do as we prepare for your dad's pastoral anniversary celebrations next month."

"Oh ok. Where is Pastor Darrick?"

"He's inside the church, still working. I'm headed home to start dinner. You have a lovely night and be careful going home."

"You too."

I press the button for the window to go back up as I watch her pull off. I wait a few more minutes before turning the truck off and going into the church.

I use the key to let myself in. I walk to the area of the offices and find Darrick sitting at his desk. He doesn't even hear me come in as he seems to be deep in thought.

I close and lock the door and he finally looks up.

"Grayce, what are you doing here?"

I don't say anything as I walk over to his desk. Being the assistant pastor of the church has its perks and one is this nice office.

I slide his chair back far enough for me to fit in. Bending over, I stick my tongue in his mouth and he takes no time sucking it. His hands start to roam my body as I let out a quiet moan.

He remembers where we are and stops.

"Grayce, stop, we cannot do this here. My wife—"

"She's gone," I tell him while unzipping his pants.

"Stop, we're in the church. We cannot do this."

I don't listen because although his mouth is saying one thing, his soldier is standing at full attention. Releasing him from his boxers, I begin to kiss the head of his penis.

"Do. You. Want. Me. To. Stop?" I ask, in between kisses.

He doesn't say a word as he lays his head on the back of the chair.

Smiling, I continue to kiss down the shaft before taking his balls into my mouth. He moans.

I slide all of him in until it reaches the back of my throat. He moans louder meaning I've hit the right spot. I move him in and out until my tongue reaches the tip, making him squirm. Pushing him back in, I go lower and lower until my lips touch the base.

I release him when I start to gag. Spitting on my hand, I begin to rub up and down with a firm grip.

"Oh God!" he moans out while looking me in the eyes.

Licking the tip, I take him back in. He grabs my head with both hands and begins pounding into my mouth. When he slows down, I remove him from my mouth and stand up.

"Damn girl, what are you trying to do to me?"

I still don't say anything as I stand and raise my skirt. Pushing his chair against the wall, I place one leg over one arm before doing the same with the other. I grab his soldier and guide him to my opening which is dripping wet.

Sliding down on him, I close my eyes, biting my lip.

He wraps his arms around my back as I begin to ride the thoughts of the day away.

"Give me what I need," I whisper in his ear.

He stands up and walks me back to the desk, sitting me on the edge. Unbuckling his pants, he lets them fall to his ankles before continuing

"Is this what you need?"

"Yes, give it to me!"

I lean back on the desk as he begins to work.

"Yes, oh, yes!"

I rise up and grab him around his neck as I grind against him.

"I'm cumm—"

A knock on the door silences me.

"Darrick, you in there?"

"Uh, yes, yes I am. One second. I didn't realize the door was locked," he says, scrambling to fix his pants while I fix my skirt and his desk.

I run over and plop down on the couch before he opens the door.

"I didn't know you were still here, is everything ... Grayce?"

"Dad," I smile.

"What are you doing here?" he asks, looking back at Darrick.

"I saw Pastor Darrick's car in the parking lot when Shaun dropped me off so I decided to come in and talk to him about the situation with Shaun and I."

"Why didn't you come and talk to me?"

"Because I wanted to get someone else's opinion and I knew he would have just what I needed."

Darrick clears his throat after hearing the last part.

"Melvin, what are you doing back? Did you forget something?" he asks my dad.

"Yea, I left my schedule for the week. I thought Gina had it."

"Do you need me to get it, Daddy?"

"Yea, that would be good. I need to speak to Pastor Darrick about something anyway," he replies, handing me his keys.

I take my time going to my dad's office to retrieve his calendar. When I return they are in deep conversation.

"Here's your calendar, Daddy. You know you wouldn't have to keep up with that if you'd get a new phone. That piece of junk you have now is so outdated."

"I don't know how to work those fancy phones nowadays but this one is playing out so I may have to let you upgrade it soon."

"I'm on spring break next week, so let's do it tomorrow."

"That's fine," he says. "Well, I'm going to go; your mother is in the car and you know how she gets. I'll see you tomorrow, baby, and Pastor Darrick, call me later tonight."

After my dad leaves, Darrick starts pacing. "That was to close."

"It was actually kind of fun."

"Fun? Are you serious?"

"Stop being so dramatic," I say grabbing my purse. "You know you enjoyed it."

"As much as I did, we cannot run the risk of being caught. Do you know what it will do to my family and my career?"

"You aren't the only one who has something to lose, Pastor Darrick," I say sarcastically. "Anyway, what did my dad want to talk to you about?"

"He was trying to find out what you and I were talking about. What's going on with you and my son?"

"You don't know? He's moving to New Orleans."

"No, he hasn't said anything. What are you going to do? Go with him?"

"No, we've decided to end our relationship."

"Oh," he says.

"I thought you'd be happy. Seeing that you've been sleeping with your son's fiancé."

"It's not that, it's just—"

"Don't worry about it, I have to go."

"Grayce?"

"Yea?"

"We can't do this again."

"Do what?"

"You know what. We can't do it here again."

I laugh, "Ok."

"I'm serious, Grayce!" he yells to my back.

I smile as I walk out of his office.

If you didn't catch it, Pastor Darrick Blair is Shaun's father but he is also the associate pastor under my daddy. I know I shouldn't be sleeping with him but hey, who's sleeping anyway? It's just a little fun.

Merci

I get home and I have the house to myself. I head to my room to get out of these clothes. I put on some lounging pants and tank. Walking down the hall, I hear the alarm chirp.

"Grayce?"

I walk into the living room as she is throwing her purse on the couch.

"Didn't you hear me call your name? Shit, I was making sure no one was trying to break in and get my stuff," I say laughing.

"No one has to break in to get what you give away so freely."

"Wow! You are one sad little girl."

"I'd rather be sad than a hoe."

"Look Grayce, go on up to your room before we both say some things we'll regret."

"I just don't understand why you can't mind your business."

"Are you still upset over lunch? Girl, grow up."

"It's not just lunch, it's everything. I am sick of the arguing with Mom and Dad and now I have the added stress of this mess with Shaun."

"And what part of any of that is my fault?"

"I'm just sick of walking in your shadow."

I start coughing like I was choking. "Did you really let that come out of your mouth? I know I didn't hear you right."

"You heard me. I am sick of having the same conversation with Mom and Dad."

"The conversations that can be avoided if you would own up to who you really are."

"Are we about to have this discussion again? You don't understand what it was like for me living under Mom and Dad's thumb after you left."

"I wouldn't have been forced to leave had you taken responsibility that night."

"I've apologized for that a hundred times."

"Yea, and for the hundredth and one time, I'm letting you know that your apology isn't sufficient enough for the hell I went through. Do you have any idea how much I suffered when it could have all been avoided by you fessing up to being the one actually having sex in the house with some boy, and not me?"

"You didn't have to leave."

"Are you serious? You saw, firsthand, what he did to me and the mere fact that you would let that come from your mouth ought to have me slapping the shit out of you. Plus it proves my point: you aren't truly sorry," I say, walking towards her. "You'll never know the feeling of worthlessness that is instilled in you by your very own dad. To have him stand over you, calling you names while kicking you like you're nothing! You've never had Dad treat you like you have a deadly disease and if he loves you, he'll catch it. You have no idea how hard it used to be for me. So don't stand there acting like you're the victim because, bitch, you are far from it!"

"I'm sorry."

"Yea, you definitely are and I should have left your ass crying on my porch a year ago. Maybe then I wouldn't have to deal with this."

I walk away from her as she starts with the fake tears again. Making it to my bedroom, I slam the door and fall back on the bed.

I start to think about that day and all the anger comes right back with the memories.

Eleven years ago

Getting out of the shower, I hear Daddy screaming my name!

"Merci, where are you? Get out here now!"

Wrapping the towel around me, I hurry out of the bathroom.

"Dad, why are you screaming?"

He instantly slaps me.

My hand flies to my face as I stand there looking at him.

"What have I told you about having boys in this house?"

"Dad, what are you talking about? I haven't had anyone in the house. I just got home so I was taking a shower," I say through the tears that are now falling.

"You're a liar. I saw a boy running from your bedroom window."

"Why do you always assume it's me when Grayce and I share a room?" I yell. "Why do you hate me so much? What have I done that makes you despise me? Daddy, I'm not the only girl in this house, yet every time something happens, I am the one who gets the blame. You think—"

Before I can finish, he slaps me again. This time it's so hard that I fall. My towel comes loose and I am lying on the floor naked while he's standing over me screaming, kicking and calling me every name but the one he gave me.

I yell for him to stop but it only makes him angrier. He continues to yell while beating me with the belt he pulled from his waist. My screams get louder.

"You're a whore!" he yells, with every hit getting harder and harder. "A filthy disgrace to this family."

"Daddy, stop it!" Grayce yells. "Stop!"

She manages to pull him off me as I roll tighter into a ball on the floor.

"You are a disgrace before God," he roars before turning to walk out the kitchen.

My sister comes over and tries to grab me. I flinch.

"Merci, it's me," she says, putting the towel over me.

I look up at her before grabbing the towel and getting up.

I don't say anything as I make my way back to our bedroom with her on my heels. I use the towel to wipe the blood from some of the places the belt connected. Flinching in pain, I go over to the dresser and grab a pair of jogging pants and a t-shirt. I begin to get dressed as she just stands at the door and watches. I put on some tennis shoes and walk over to my closet and grab a duffle bag.

"What are you doing?"

"Packing."

"Where are you going?"

"Why do you care?"

"Merci—"

"Don't you dare," I say with my hand up. "You stood there and let him beat the hell out of me for something you did."

"I'm sorry."

I turn and continue throwing things in my bag. I go to our bathroom and get my toiletries before returning to the bedroom.

I grab my purse, my duffle bag and my keys. I hear my dad in his office as I head towards the front door.

Once I make it to my car I throw my stuff in, start it and don't look back.

I pull over a few blocks from the house to get myself together, trying to figure out the 'what's next' part. I have money saved from my grandparents and the two summers I worked so I know I'll be fine. My saving grace is a full scholarship to Tennessee State University, which means I have a place to stay.

The downside, I'm not due to leave for another three days so I'll have to find somewhere to stay. One thing for sure, I'm not going back to my parents. I stop and gas up my car before hitting the highway. I find a dump of a hotel that doesn't ask for ID and pay for three nights. Afterwards, I move into my dorm and begin my new life.

Whew, Lord! Snapping out of those memories, I shake my head while wiping away tears that are now streaming down my face. Leaving that house, when I did, changed everything, including our relationship. It was never the same after that, especially with Grayce. I didn't go home and we only talked on the phone some holidays. They weren't invited to my college graduation and the only way they found out I was back in Memphis was because someone else told them.

This is why I don't know what I was thinking when I allowed Grayce to move in with me. When she showed up on my doorstep almost a year ago, begging and crying for me to let her stay, I should have slammed the door hard enough to shake the windows but I didn't. *Worst mistake of my life!*

Grayce

March

I get up the next morning, thankful to be a teacher because spring break means no work. Sitting up in the bed, I remember the argument with Merci and it reminds me of the things I need to do today, starting with finding my own place to live.

I grab my computer and begin browsing through the houses on Zillow. I find one in Olive Branch that looks promising so I call about it. I make plans to meet the realtor at two.

Scratching that off my list, I get a reminder that I'm supposed to take Dad to upgrade his phone. I call him to see if he will change his mind again, like he has so many times before.

"Hello."

"Hey Daddy, you haven't changed your mind, have you?"

He laughs while saying, "No Grayce. I know I have to 'get with the program', as you young people say!"

I laugh. "Ok Daddy, are you ready? I can be there to pick you up in thirty minutes."

"I'll be ready."

"And Daddy, wear something casual. This is your off day, no suit allowed."

He grunts before hanging up the call.

Three hours and a headache later, we finally leave the store with an upgraded phone but not before looking at every one they had! I take Dad home and it couldn't have been fast enough for me and my nerves.

Shit! It's almost two. I plug the address into my GPS and realize I can still make it on time.

Getting out of the car, I meet Bill, the realtor, who shows me around the house.

"This is a very nice home," I say once we are back in the great room.

"The owners have kept it up quite nicely. All of the appliances have been updated and it was recently painted and new carpet installed."

"Great. I'll look over the paperwork and I'll let you know by the end of the week."

"Here's my card. Call me with any questions."

Getting in my truck, there are so many things going on in my mind. Am I really ready to move out? How am I going to handle this situation with Shaun? On top of that, I don't think I can even afford the rent on this place by myself. *Damn it!*

I unlock my glove compartment and pull out my trusty sidekick as I scroll to find the number I'm looking for and send a text.

'Hey I really could use your hands on me.'

Before I can put the phone down his response comes through.

'Oh yea? I'm free now.'

'Good. Meet me at the Homewood Suites on Goodman across from JCPenney. I'll text you the room.'

His response, 'I'll meet you there in fifteen minutes.'

I feel like dancing in my seat hoping this man knows how to work my body like nobody's business because that's just what I am in need of today.

I pull into the front of the hotel and almost jump out before cutting the car off.

"Girl, get it together," I laugh while speaking to myself.

I go in and get a room for the night. Back at the truck, I send a quick text before parking and grabbing my purse.

I take a shower and wrap a towel around me just as the knock I've been waiting for comes. I open the door and when I see him, I step back and drop the towel.

He rushes in and pushes me against the wall.

"Damn, I couldn't wait to get here," he says, roughly kissing me all over my neck.

"I like it when you play rough!"

"Shut up and turn around," he commands, and I am happy to oblige.

Reaching down to grab the buckle on his pants, he smacks my hand. "If I needed help I would have asked for it!"

He drops to his knees and his lips are roaming all over my body.

"Please," I say.

"Please what, Grayce?"

"Stop teasing me! Please…"

"Then tell me what you want."

"I want you to… Ooh umm… I want you to… I want you to… shit!"

"Say it, Grayce. What do you want me to do to you?"

"I want to feel you. Please, I need you to make love to me! Please!"

He slowly gets up and leads me to the bed, pushing me on it while he starts removing his clothes.

"Baby please… I beg."

He climbs on top of me, covering my mouth with his as he begins to kiss me so deep I can't tell where his lips start and mine end. By the time he releases, I have tears streaming down my face.

"Baby, what's wrong? Do you want me to stop?"

"No, don't stop. Make love to me."

And he does just that until we both collapse back on the bed.

"Shit!" I jump up realizing it's dark outside. I move quickly, looking for my clothes and my phone, knowing I will never hear the end of this from my sister! I don't even remember falling to sleep. I look over on the night stand and realize I've been asleep for hours!

"Grayce, come back to bed!"

"I can't, I have to get home. I'm sure my parents have been calling nonstop to see where I am."

"Damn, how old are you?"

"Look, don't start, ok, not tonight. I'm tired and I need to get home," I say, walking back to him. "And I don't need to hear Merci's mouth."

"Forget her."

"You weren't saying that when you were trying to get in her bed."

"Well, I got you instead, and if I'm not mistaken, you came up to me in the store, remember?"

"You know she's going to kill me if she ever finds out."

"Who's going to tell her? The cat has my tongue." He snatches me by the arm, pulling me back into the bed.

"Justice, I can't," I say as he rolls on top of me, taking my nipple into his mouth. "I've got to—oh!"

"You were saying?" he asks, moving down to my little lady, who is eagerly awaiting his tongue. "I can't hear you?"

"Nothing! Don't stop!"

Merci

"No Mother dear, I do not know where your precious Grayce is."

Why in the hell did I answer the freaking phone?

"Yes, I am still here but the answer is still the same: I don't know where she is and you asking again won't change that!" I say, raising my voice.

I hear the alarm chirp and just when I am about to repeat myself again I see Grayce standing in the living room mouthing for me not to tell Mom she's here.

Laughing, I say, "Yes Mother that was the alarm you heard."

Rolling my eyes while wanting to hit my head against the wall, I go on, "If it was Grayce, don't you think I would have told you? Hell, I wish it was so you can get off my phone."

She yells that this conversation is useless.

"You're right, but I do believe you called my phone, ma'am. You can hang up at any time."

After she swears, she says to have a good day. "I will, and you have a great day as well," I reply.

"Damn!" I yell, putting my phone on the counter as I finish fixing my coffee.

I look up to see Grayce trying to exit stage left.

"No you don't, heifer! I've been on the phone with your mother for over thirty minutes and you think you're going to just walk away?"

"Merci, I am not in the mood, ok?"

"And do you think I am in the mood to deal with the same question of where you are every time you don't answer your freaking phone? You are a grown ass woman who is still afraid of her parents."

"I am not afraid of them."

"Then why not answer your phone? Or were you to busy getting your back tilted?"

"Don't start. I was not out having sex. Unlike you, I am not a whore."

"Are you sure about that, oh sister of mine? What is it the bible says? Um, something like, before you talk about the speck in my eye remove the one from yours."

"What are you talking about?"

"Your shirt, saved one, it's on inside out!"

"Merci, I…"

"Girl bye, your walk of shame is waiting."

But I'm the hoe... right?

Grayce

Shit! Shit! How in the hell did I put my shirt on backwards? Damn it to hell!

Before I can even get in my room good, my phone is vibrating again.

"Hello Mom."

"Grayce, are you ok? I've been calling you all night. We were beginning to think something happened. Have we done or said something because if we did just say it, you—"

Before she can finish… "Mom, MOM! I'm fine. I forgot to put my phone on the charger last night and I didn't realize it was dead until I came back from a walk this morning. And I saw Dad yesterday, remember?"

"I know but you never ignore my calls. Are you sure everything is ok? I know with Shaun leaving it must be a lot for you to deal with but maybe you can change your mind and go with him? Yawl can get married before you leave with a small ceremony at the church."

"That would be the ideal thing for you and Daddy but we've already discussed this. I am not getting married to Shaun. I know you all handpicked him and thought he was what's best for me, but he isn't. This move to New Orleans was a blessing in disguise."

"Well, excuse us for wanting more for you, little girl. Your dad and I don't want you to turn out like your sister but it looks like it's too late. All we ever wanted is for you to find a good wholesome boy you can have some babies with, but I guess it's too much."

"Mom, I'm sorry. I didn't mean for it to come out like it did but it's still true. While I appreciate everything you and Daddy have done, it's time for me to make the decisions regarding my life."

"Fine Grayce, but don't you dare come running back to us to fix it when it doesn't work out like you think it will."

"Mommy—"

"Goodbye Grayce."

I turn to lay my phone down and see Merci. "Shit girl, you scared the crap out of me standing there being nosey!"

"How can I be nosey in my own freaking house? Anyway, you go girl!" she says, clapping her hands. "Whoever you were with last night must have laid it down on you good."

"What are you talking about? No one laid anything on me."

"Girl, you can keep up with that lie if you want but only some good d—"

"Merci, don't you dare!"

Laughing, she says, "You've heard the word 'dick' before. Hell, it was that good dick that caused you to talk to your mother like that! I mean—"

"You mean what, Merci? Huh… what do you mean? Can you just leave? Don't you have to be at work or something?"

"Don't get mad at me trick, I was just stating the obvious, but whatever!"

Ughhh!

Closing the door I slide down to the floor and begin to pray.

"Lord, I just need you to help me even if it's a little bit. I don't know how much more of this I can take. I'm lost and I need your help. God, my life is in a downward spiral and I need you. You said all I had to do was ask so here I am asking, begging you to help me. Give me the strength to be who it is you would have me to be and to do what you would have me to do because I know this is not it! I know I've failed you and I'm sorry, please forgive me. Oh God, please forgive me for all the things I've done to my sister. I've caused her to hate me and I deserve it but I'm tired of fighting. I'm tired of fighting her and my parents. Lord, I was supposed to be my sister's keeper but all I've ever kept is secrets and lies. I'm sorry and I'm ashamed. Can you please move her heart to forgive me? I know that most of the pain in her heart is because of me and I'm sorry. Will you please, oh God, help me to make it right before it is too late? God please… please hear my prayer…"

Merci

Standing on the outside of Grayce's door I hear her crying and praying. I don't know if I believe her because she's become so good at lying but she sounds sincere. Yes, I want to forgive her but I have so much hurt and resentment in my heart that I can't... *Can I?*

I shake it off and head downstairs to leave for work. I still have the sound of her praying in my head and I begin to feel guilty. Can I forgive her? Can we build a better relationship? I did let her move in, so I can if I want, but do I? Should I?

I have all these thoughts in my head but then I get mad at myself for feeling guilty. Hell, I wasn't the one who caused the rift between us so why should I feel this way? She was the one that did this! Not me! Why am I feeling bad? *Shit!*

Forget this, I don't have a reason to feel bad. Yes, I hope she gets the deliverance and forgiveness she needs from God because I ain't about that life right now. I'm well aware of what the bible says and I'll probably forgive her one day, but it's not today.

I grab my things to head out. I stop by Republic Coffee for a quick bite to eat. It's not on my usual route but I needed something to take my mind off this thang with Grayce. As I am walking in, Justice is walking out.

"Well, well," he says.

I just look at him.

"How are you doing, Merci?"

"I am just fine, Justice," I say walking off.

"Oh, a brother can't get any conversation? I haven't seen you since the night you kicked me out of your house." He laughs.

"Yes, I am aware. What can I do for you?"

"Dang, it's like that?"

"I don't have time for this."

"It's cool, I was messing with you. It was good seeing you again though, you're still fine as ever. Maybe we can hook up and you can give me another one of those night caps like before."

"Nah, I'm good."

"Are you sure?"

"Very."

"Well, to bad but tell your sister I said hello and that I can still taste her in my mouth."

When he walks off, it resonates what he said. No, he must have been talking about the night he kissed her. It has to be. Either way, I'll find out.

=====

A few days later, I wake up still thinking about Grayce. As I prepare myself for work, I cannot get her out of my head. As much as she gets on my nerves, and although I want to hate her, I know I have to forgive her.

Walking by the mirror for one last look, I stop. Looking at the reflection in the mirror, I know I have my faults but this thing with Grayce, I don't know.

As I am walking out of the bathroom, I hear *'You have to forgive her,'* as if someone is in the room with me. I look around just to be sure I am not crazy. When I don't see anyone, I shake it off. Heading down the hall, I grab my purse, briefcase and keys and reach for the door. It won't open. *What the hell?*

I try the door again and it's as if it's dead bolted from the outside. I hear it again, *'You have to forgive her.'* I close my eyes and say out loud, "I hear you Lord, you're right and I will eventually." I try the door again and again it won't budge. "Ok!" I scream, "I'll do it today."

This time when I turn the knob on the door, it opens just fine. I close it, open it again, and it opens. I laugh because God has a way of getting your attention.

I decide to stop for breakfast at one of my favorite eateries, Bae Bae's Girls. Making my way inside, I head to my usual table.

"Hey Merci, you having your usual?" the waitress says.

"Hey Shay, yes, that will be great. Where is everybody, it's quiet this morning?"

"No, you happened to miss the rush. I'll be back with your coffee."

Grabbing a copy of the daily newspaper, I settle in as Shay places the coffee in front of me.

"Excuse me, miss, excuse me," someone says, tapping me on my shoulder.

"Oh I am sorry, I wasn't paying attention. Can I help you?" I say looking up.

"No, let me apologize for disturbing you. I just wanted to speak and tell you that you are beautiful."

Blushing and smirking, I reply, "Umm huh, is that the best you got?"

"I, um, it's just—" he says equally blushing.

"I was kidding. Thank you Mr…"

"Harvey, but please call me Thomas."

"Thomas, thank you for the compliment."

"I don't mean to be so forward but would it be alright if I joined you for breakfast Mrs…"

"It's Ms. Alexander, but you can call me Merci, and yes, please have a seat."

We sit and talk over coffee until our breakfast is brought out. Before long I glance at the clock and realize that we have been talking for an hour and I am late for work.

"Thomas, while this has been great I really have to get to work."

"I have to do the same but I would love to get to know you better and maybe take you out for dinner?"

"That would be great."

He pays the bill and we head to the door "Thank you for my breakfast, I really enjoyed talking to you." Reaching into my purse, I pull out a card and hand it to him. "Call me when you're ready for dinner."

"Now, don't act like you don't know me when I call you."

"I won't, I'm looking forward to it. Have a great day, Mr. Harvey."

"You do the same, Ms. Alexander."

I smile all the way to my freaking car. Dude was fine as heck and I learned during the conversation that he has no kids, his own car, a job and he's saved. Thank you Jesus. Getting into my car, reality hits and I say out loud, "Girl, stop getting ahead of yourself, you don't know that man from a can of paint."

Bucking my seat belt, I think about it and suddenly shout, "But I plan to!"

By the time I walk into my office, I am all smiles.

"Good Morning Ms. Alexander, something has you happy today."

"Good morning Rhonda. I'm just blessed and I know it and not ashamed to show it."

"I hear that!"

"Is there anything pressing I need to address?"

"No, in fact your calendar is clear until after lunch. Do you want to go over some of the files that are closing this month?"

"Um, no, you should be fine to close them out. I have some research to do on a new client but if you need me, let me know."

After working for a few hours, Rhonda buzzes.

"Ms. Alexander, your sister is on line one."

"Lord, my day was going so good," I whisper. "Thanks Rhonda."

"Yes, Grayce?"

"Hey, you busy?"

"I am at work. What can I do for you?"

"Merci, can you please drop the attitude? I called to see if maybe you wanted to do lunch today?"

I pull the receiver from my ear because this trick must have been in my liquor cabinet.

"Hello, Merci, you there?"

"Yeah, I'm here trying to figure out if you're drunk or not."

"I'm serious. I've been thinking and I realize time is too short to continue the way we've been. I want my sister back."

I laugh. "Hell, you're just realizing that. We haven't treated each other like sisters in years so why start now? What do you really want? Have you done something to my house?"

She lets out a breath. "All I want to do is to have lunch and talk to you without the arguing and name calling. Can you please do this one thing for me? Please, Merci?"

"Fine, but if it is anything more I'm leaving! I don't have time for foolishness today."

"It's not, I promise. How about Olive Garden at 1:30?"

"Fine. I'll see you then."

Lord, you're tripping; for real! But if this is you, set a guard over my mouth because I know not what this girl is gone come with today! Amen.

Grayce

I am a nervous wreck waiting on Merci to come in. I don't know why I am even bothering to talk to her because I know she's not going to forgive me.

"Ok, I'm here, let's get this over with," she says slamming her purse into the booth.

"Dammit Merci, why do you always have an attitude with me? If you didn't want to be here, then you shouldn't have come. I thought maybe we could talk, for once without being at each other's throat, but if you don't want to then fine, just go!"

"Ok, pipe down with all the dramatics, I'll stay!"

After a few moments of silence, I add, "I ordered you a sweet tea, is that ok?"

"Yea, that's fine."

The waitress comes back with our drinks and we place our orders. Once she leaves, I nervously start talking.

"Merci, I asked you to lunch today because there's some things I need to say to you."

"Ok, I'm listening."

"I'm sorry."

"Grayce—"

"Please let me get this out. Growing up, I can remember it always being the two of us but somewhere along the way the relationship we once had got lost—"

"It didn't get lost, it got destroyed," she interrupts.

I look at her.

"Sorry, go ahead."

"Yes, our relationship was destroyed and I know it was mainly my fault and I'm deeply sorry. I never should have taken advantage of the way Daddy treated you. I knew when I got in trouble Daddy would blame you and I let him. Yes, I should have spoken up but my selfishness wouldn't let me and I am so sorry. Merci, you have to believe me when I tell you that. You always had my back and I should've had yours, been my sister's keeper. Can you please forgive me? I know I've apologized so many times but this time I asked God to forgive me first and He has. I know you may not be able to do it right now but I hope at some point you will. I really miss you."

She doesn't say anything as I wipe the tears streaming down my face.

"Merci, say something please."

"I don't know what to say."

"Say anything! Tell me to go to hell, tell me you'll think about it, or even say you won't; just say something!"

Merci starts to cry.

"I didn't mean to make you cry," I say, handing her the napkin.

"Don't ever think my tears are because of you. I cry because I'm angry at myself for how long I've allowed the drama of this family to consume me. I realize that my family is a bunch of liars and it caused me to hate you, Grayce. Do you hear me?" she says, hitting the table. "I hated my own baby sister with everything in me. And it's crazy because then I allowed you to move in with me. I don't know why, maybe it was God's doing. All I know is, I've spent too many sleepless nights trying to understand what I ever did to be treated the way you, Mom and Dad treat me. And I'm tired. Do you have any idea the times I've wanted to share my life with you? Or the many nights I wanted to call my only sister when something good happened to me? Do you?"

"I'm so sorry," I tell her. "Please forgive me."

"I want to but what's to stop you from hurting me again?"

"All I can do is promise you that I won't. Can you at least try?"

"I'm tired, Grayce. Really tired and I don't want to do this anymore."

"I understand. We can go—"

"No, I mean I don't want to hold on to this anger anymore. It's destroying me. I have to forgive you in order to move on with my life. It's not going to be overnight but I'm willing to try."

The waitress arrives with our entrees. Before taking a bite, Grayce says, "I'm truly sorry and I will spend the rest of my life making this up to you."

"Don't do that. I don't need you making anything up to me because my life has been good. But I did hear you praying the other day and as much as I wanted to just walk away I couldn't. Hearing you made me realize I need to do the same. I understand now that in order for me to open myself up to be loved, I have to first forgive you and move on. I didn't think it would be this soon but it is. Now, all I ask is that you give me time to rebuild the relationship."

"I can do that."

We both release breaths and smile. It's the first time in a long time that we actually smile at each other and mean it. *At least, I hope so.*

We eat and get ready to part ways.

"Thank you for coming Merci. This lunch meant more than you know."

"I'm glad I came. We've never had an opportunity to hang out as adults so thank you for lunch. I'll see you at home."

Once she leaves, I realize I don't have anything else to do since I'm on spring break. So I figure I'll stop down at the church.

=====

"Hey Daddy."

"Grayce, what are you doing here? Were we supposed to be doing something?"

"No, I just left lunch with Merci and I didn't have anything else to do."

He rolls his eyes.

"Why are you rolling your eyes?"

"I don't know why you insist on staying with that girl. She is a bad influence."

"Daddy, please don't start. She is my sister and your daughter and I miss having a relationship with her."

"Why do you need to have a relationship with someone who sleeps around with any and everybody?"

"You don't know that and stop saying it. Tell me, why do you hate her so much? What did she ever do to you?"

"I don't hate her, but I hate her ways."

"It sure doesn't seem that way and it still doesn't explain why you treat her so bad."

"It's not worth talking about."

"It is, Daddy. Everything was great between all of us until I was about thirteen then something happened and you could no longer stand Merci. What was it?"

"I don't want to talk about it!" he yells, which scares me.

I look at him.

"Why are you looking at me like that?"

"Because you're starting to scare me. I don't know what happened but I am ashamed of the way we've treated her and it needs to stop. She's your daughter."

He doesn't say anything as I stand up to leave. I go over and hug him.

"I hope you get the opportunity to ask for forgiveness before it's too late, Daddy. Time isn't standing still for us to get it right, you know."

Just then there's a knock on the door.

"Come in," Dad says. "Pastor Blair, what can I do for you?"

"I apologize, I didn't mean to interrupt. Grayce, it's nice to see you." He hugs me.

"It's good to see you too, Reverend."

"Have you talked to my son?"

"Not in a few days. I know he's busy with the move."

"Yea, I hate that you and Shaun didn't work. I was looking forward to having you as a daughter-in-law."

"Well, things happens for a reason. It was good seeing you again. I'll let you guys get back to work. I'll talk to you later Daddy."

Merci

A few weeks later - April

I'm up getting ready for church when Grayce comes through the door and sits on my bathroom counter. Our relationship isn't 100% great but it is getting better.

"What's up, Grayce?"

"Nothing."

"You're lying, what do you want?"

"Can I go to church with you today?"

I drop my comb as I turn to look at her.

"Stop playing. You know you aren't missing a Sunday at the beloved Bishop, Dr. Pastor Melvin Alexander's church."

"I'm serious, Merci."

"Fine, but you better be ready in thirty minutes."

She jumps down and runs out my room to finish getting dressed.

Forty-five minutes later, we pull up into the parking lot of Rock Church of Southaven.

"Wow, this is a nice church."

"It is and I think you're going to love the service."

We head in and I make my way to my usual section. Speaking to the members, they are all shocked to see Grayce with me. They've heard of her although they've never met her.

As we take our seat the Praise Team rises. After a few selections, they end with the song, 'Put a praise on it,' by Tasha Cobbs.

One of the associate ministers gets up and goes through the preliminaries of service and we get to fellowship period.

"Merci, it is so good to see you this morning. This has got to be your sister, Grayce?"

"Yes it is. Grayce, this is our First Lady, Joy Parker."

"It's so nice to finally meet you. Merci has told us wonderful things about you," she says, giving her a hug.

"It's nice to meet you too."

"I hope this won't be the last time you visit us."

"It won't, you all have an amazing church."

After the many introductions and hugs, we take our seats. Grayce looks like something is bothering her so I lean over to her, "Are you alright?"

"Yea, yes, I'm fine."

I don't pay any mind to it as Pastor Nathan Parker stands at the podium. He begins reading from Genesis 2:16-17, speaking on the subject of 'Results of sin'.

"In Genesis 1, we read about the creation of Heaven and Earth. We walk through the many things God created in a barren land and we see that His work is good. In Genesis 2, after all the work is done and inspected, God rests and He blesses this day, the seventh day as Holy. After resting He continues with creation and creates man, in His image, from the dust of the ground; He creates the Garden of Eden, rivers and more fruit-bearing trees.

"He places the man within the garden and gives Him a specific warning saying, 'You may freely eat the fruit of every tree in the garden — except the tree of the knowledge of good and evil. If you eat its fruit, you are sure to die.'

"God then creates woman from the man's rib, leaves them in Eden, naked and unashamed. Oh but then Genesis 3 begins to be written and here we see, for the first time, a serpent. Bible says he's the shrewdest, meaning he was smarter and more mischievous than the other animals. He approaches Eve, knowing she will be the easiest to convince because for one, God didn't tell Eve not to eat of the tree, He told Adam. And two, the serpent had probably already spoken to Eve in order for her to now be comfortable enough to converse with him here.

"The more the serpent talks, the more the wheels of doubt are turning in Eve's mind. She isn't thinking about the consequences they may face; her only thought now is to see if what the serpent is saying is actually true. In other words, she's saying 'I'll take my chance and deal with the penalty later.' And she does. She eats from the tree and not only that, she gives Adam some and he eats it too. And it is then their eyes are open and we begin to see the results of sin. For sin is defined as an immoral act considered to be a transgression against divine law."

As Pastor Parker continues to preach, Grayce hangs on to his every word.

After service, I introduce her to him before we leave. As we are walking out, she is extremely quiet. I wait until we get in the car to inquire.

"Grayce, what's wrong. You've been different since I introduced you to First Lady Parker. Did I miss something?"

She starts to cry.

"Girl, what's wrong? Talk to me."

"Everybody here acted like they already knew me. They weren't shocked to see you had a sister."

"Why would they be?"

"I didn't think you'd talk about me because of the way our relationship has been. Not here anyway."

"You have to understand something. This has been my family for the past five years. They love me with all my flaws and they don't judge. So it's only right they know about you. Regardless of the situation, you are my family, Grayce."

"I'm so sorry for everything I've done to you," she says in between sobs.

I reach into the door of my car to find a napkin.

"Grayce, stop crying. We've been through all of this."

"I just can't believe how bad I allowed things to get between us. I—"

I get out the car and go around to her side, open the door and pull her into my arms. I don't say anything, I just let her cry.

By the time I look up, Pastor Parker and his wife are right beside us.

Taking Grayce and me by the hand, he says, "Forgiveness is taking one step at a time with the sole intentions of forgiving and forgetting. Whatever happened in the past, leave it there." He takes a pace back from us. "Now, take the first step of forgiveness today but only if you desire to leave here free."

I look at her and she looks at me and we take the step together.

Smiling, I hug her and then turn to hug Pastor Parker. He whispers in my ear, "Leave here free, Merci."

"I will. Thank you Pastor."

After hugging his wife, we get back in the car.

"Look what you did, you made me mess up my makeup," I say, laughing.

"I know. Now we both look a mess."

"How are you going to explain this to your parents at brunch today?"

"I'm not."

"You know they're not going to leave you alone until you do."

"Not today because I am not going to lunch with them. Let's go downtown and eat."

"Are you sure?"

"Yes, I'm positive."

"Ok den," I say as I start the car.

Grayce

Sitting at lunch, laughing with Merci, I begin to feel sick.

"Grayce, are you ok?"

"Yea, I'm good."

"Are you sure, you don't look to good."

"I'm going to the bathroom."

"Do you need me to go with you?"

I don't answer as I am running into the bathroom. I barely make it to the toilet before my entire lunch comes back up.

"Grayce?" Merci calls out.

I grab some tissue to wipe my mouth. Flushing the toilet, I open the door to find her standing there with a look of concern on her face.

"Grayce, what's wrong Are you okay?" she asks, handing me a wet paper towel.

"Yea, the salmon didn't agree with me," I reply, walking over to wash my hands and rinse my mouth.

She doesn't say anything.

"Merci, I'm fine."

"Grayce, are you pregnant?"

"Hell no!"

"Then let me take you to urgent care, it could be food poisoning."

"I don't need that, I'm fine," I say, staggering as I begin to feel lightheaded.

She catches me. "Grayce, you are not fine. I'm taking you to the Minor Med."

=====

Making it home after two hours at the Minor Medical Clinic, I'm exhausted.

"Merci."

"You don't owe me an explanation. I was just making sure you were fine," she replies walking down the hall.

I drop my bags and go upstairs to my bedroom. I close the door, fall across the bed and cry myself to sleep.

I wake up with a hell of a headache and with the same clothes I had on yesterday. I search for my phone and call my principal letting her know I can't come in today.

Taking off my clothes, I get into the shower and let the warmness of the water fall over my entire body. I shampoo my hair and finally get out.

Putting on my robe, I wipe off the mirror and realize my eyes are red and swollen. Combing through my hair, I leave it down as I go downstairs for some ibuprofen.

Making it into the kitchen, I smell bacon and coffee and I instantly feel nauseous.

"You aren't going to work today?" Merci asks as I bolt for the bathroom.

Coming back into the kitchen, I sit down at the island.

"I'm guessing it's a no for work and for bacon, huh?"

"Merci, what am I going to do?"

"First off, take these," she says, handing me two Tylenols and orange juice. "Second, here's some ginger tea I got from the store this morning. I read that it helps with morning sickness."

I begin to cry.

"Girl, stop crying. You are a grown ass woman."

"Who's pregnant. What am I going to do?"

"Either have it or you don't."

"Dad is going to kill me."

"Fuck Dad! What do you want to do?"

"I don't know."

"Well, you don't have long to decide."

"I know."

"Whatever you decide, you need to first make a doctor's appointment, just to make sure."

"I will, this morning. Will you go with me?"

"You sure you want me there?"

"Yes, I need you there."

"What about the baby's daddy? Have you told him?"

"Not yet. I'll decide once I figure out what I'm going to do."

"Ok," she says.

"Why aren't you asking me who the daddy is?" I ask her.

"It's none of my business Grayce. When you're ready to tell me, you will. I'm headed to work. Call me if you need me, and drink that tea."

Merci

I walk into the office to find my assistant waiting for me.

"Good Morning, Ms. Alexander."

"Good morning Rhonda, what's wrong?"

"Mrs. Glassor needs to see you."

"Already?"

"Yes ma'am, she says it's urgent."

"Ok, thanks. Can you put my bags in my office?"

"Sure. Do you want me to make you a cup of coffee?"

"No thanks, I'll make it when I get back."

Walking to the elevators, I decide to take the stairs up the two floors. Opening the door, I run right into Mrs. Glassor's assistant, Sydney, who happens to be carrying a glass of juice that spills all over my shirt and skirt.

"Shit!" I yell before I can stop myself.

"Ms. Alexander, I'm so sorry!" he says, watching as the juice soaks my sheer shirt. "Oh my God, I am so sorry."

I look at him and see that he's more focused on my lace bra, which can now be clearly seen, than he is on the mess.

"Um Sydney, can you get me some napkins please?"

He finally brings his eyes to meet mine before walking to the break room. I try to shake the remnants of the liquid from my shirt and jacket as Mrs. Glassor opens her office door.

"Sydney, what is all the noise? Oh God, Merci are you alright?"

"Yes, it was an accident," I tell her as he comes back with a towel.

"Ms. Alexander, I'm—"

"Don't you dare apologize again; it was not your fault. I wasn't looking when I came through the door and it's just juice, it'll come out," I say grabbing his arm. "Seriously, it's alright." I pull my jacket close so that he can concentrate. "Mrs. Glassor, you wanted to see me?" I ask, focusing on her.

"It can wait, go and change clothes."

"No, it's fine. Is everything alright?"

"Please, come in."

Following her into the office, I close the door as she gets settled behind her desk. Handing me a file she says, "Merci, I need you to handle something for me."

"Ok, what is it and is it legal?"

She chuckles. "Yes, it's legal but there's a problem. Someone has been embezzling money from my company. I haven't had the chance to really dig deep into it because I've been preparing for my overseas trip, but I can tell you, the numbers just aren't adding up."

"Ok, wow. Do you know who it is?"

"No. I have some suspicions but I need more proof."

"What do you need me to do?"

"I need you to investigate but you'll have to go to New York to do it."

"New York?"

"Yes, because it's coming from that location."

"I see."

"Will it be a problem for you? I wouldn't ask if it wasn't a real emergency. I would investigate it myself but I'm due to fly out in two days to India and I cannot reschedule. And you are the only inside person I can trust with this."

"Mrs. Glassor, don't you worry. I'll do whatever you need to ensure we catch whoever it is. How soon will I need to be there?"

"I was hoping you'd be able to be in the office next Monday because the person I suspect will be on vacation for two weeks."

"That's not a problem but I may need a few days off this week to get some things together."

"That's not a problem. It actually works well because I have some reports running from my offsite data files that should help you. I'll have them sent over to you by Friday. I'll have Sydney make all your arrangements. I'll send a notice around letting everyone know that you'll be filling in for the general manager who is going with me to India."

"Sounds like a plan."

"Great. I knew I could count on you."

"Always, and I will keep you updated so don't worry."

"Thanks Merci. Now go home and change those clothes. I'll be out of the office for the next three weeks but if you need me in the meantime, call my cell."

"I will. Have a safe trip."

I leave her office and I decide to take the elevator this time to avoid any more accidents like the one before. I take a moment and go over things with Rhonda, letting her know I'll be out of the office for a few weeks. I grab my computer bag and purse and head out.

As soon as I get into the car my phone rings with my parents' ringtone. I don't even bother to answer it. It rings again. *UGH!* I press the button to answer it in the car.

"Hello."

"Merci, have you heard from your sister?" Mom yells.

"Mom, why are you yelling?" I ask, turning down the volume.

"Your sister isn't at work and I've tried calling her phone and she won't answer."

I laugh. "Mother, Grayce is a grown woman and if she doesn't want to answer her phone, she is entitled. And I am tired of these calls from you. Let that girl grow up!"

"Look, little girl, have you heard from her or not?"

"No and don't call me again."

"Don't—"

I don't even give her time to respond before I release the call. I do not have time for this foolishness, not today.

Arriving at the house, I hit the garage door opener. Parking, I grab my things and hop out.

I walk in to find Grayce in the kitchen.

"Hey, what are you doing back home already? Oh my God, what happened to your shirt?" she says when she turns around to see me.

"I ran into my boss's assistant who happened to be carrying a tray of juice."

"Wow. Did it mess up your skirt?"

"Nah, and it's only juice; it'll come out. Anyway, I have to go to New York for work."

"Really? When are you leaving?"

"Next week. Did you make a doctor's appointment?"

"Yes, tomorrow at ten. Will you be able to go?"

"Yea, I took off the rest of the week," I reply as my phone rings with an unknown number.

"This is Merci." I answer.

"Hey, this is Thomas. Did I catch you at a bad time?"

"No, but hold on a second," I say, taking the phone from my ear. "Um, little sister you need to call your mother, she's looking for you."

"She called you again?"

"Yea."

"Damn, will they ever stop?"

I laugh while walking to my room.

"I apologize for keeping you on hold."

"It's no problem. I will hold for you any day."

"Oh God! Please tell me it's been a while since you've dated because you have some of the lamest lines."

Laughing, he says, "It's that bad?"

"It's that bad."

"Yes, it's been a long time. I'm sorry."

"No need to apologize, we will have to work on that. Now, Mr. Harvey, what can I do for you?"

"I was hoping you'd join me for dinner tonight."

"Tonight?"

"If it's not too much of a problem. I have some time off and wanted to see you again."

"Umm, I hear you."

"I promise that's all it is."

"I'm messing with you. I would love to have dinner with you. Where and what time?"

"How about Stoney River at seven?"

"I'll be there."

"Great, can I pick you up?"

"No, I'll meet you there; let's say at the bar."

"Sounds like a plan. I look forward to seeing you."

I hang up, smiling as I go back down the hall to check on Grayce.

Grayce

God give me strength.

"Hello."

"Mom, Merci said you called looking for me. Is everything ok?"

"Yeah now that you've called. Girl, I've been calling you all day. You know how I am when you don't answer my calls. What's going on? Have we done anything to you?"

Sighing, I reply, "No. Just because I don't answer my phone, it doesn't mean I am mad at you or Dad. I was busy. Plus, it's only eleven in the morning."

"Why aren't you at work? Are you sick?"

"I have a headache, that's all, and how did you know I wasn't at work?"

"It doesn't matter. Do you need me to bring you anything? I can be there in thirty minutes."

"No Mother, I am fine. I was about to lay down."

"Are you sure?" she asks.

"Yes."

"Well, have you spoken with Shaun by any chance?"

"Shaun? No, why?"

"I thought maybe you would have given some thought to what I said about moving with him? You know he's leaving on Friday, don't you?"

Oh God, here we go!

"No Mom, I haven't talked to Shaun and I don't plan on it. Yes, I know when he's leaving and we've already had this discussion too many times to count and I'm tired of it."

"I'm just making sure you are making the best decision?"

"This is the best decision, for me. Shaun and I are in different places in our lives and we each want something that neither one of us can offer the other, so would you please leave it alone."

"Well, excuse me for wanting the best for my daughter."

"I appreciate that Mom but I am grown and I don't need you taking care of my love life."

"Fine! I really don't know what has gotten into you lately. I guess your father was right about Merci rubbing off on you. I can't believe you are giving up on a good man like Shaun and for what? To turn out like your good for nothing sister?"

"Oh. My. Freaking. God! Mother, really? You are so dramatic! Do you know how ridiculous its sounds when you and Daddy talk about MY sister rubbing off on me? Maybe if you both were to stop treating her like shit and actually take the time to get to know YOUR daughter you'd see she is not the monster yawl have made her out to be."

"I can't believe you're talking to me like this. And over someone who shut you completely out of her life for years. What has happened? Are you drinking whatever she is?"

"Are you hearing yourself? This is your damn daughter, for God sakes, and you act like she's an alien from another planet. I love my sister, and by the grace of God she still loves me. Although I don't know why, she has forgiven me and I will not let you or Daddy come between us anymore. I just pray you have a chance to make it right with her before it's too late. And another thing. I am not giving up on a good man: I am giving up a man you and Daddy chose for me, there's a difference."

"I don't even know who you are right now, Grayce. You don't sound like my daughter."

"I am the Grayce I should have been years ago instead of the one you made me into and I will no longer apologize for that."

"Listen, I'm going to let you go because you are talking foolish. Call me tomorrow when you feel better because apparently—"

Laughing, I interrupt. "You know what, Mom, I love you and hope you have a good day."

I turn around to see Merci standing behind me with her mouth open. 'Damn it, Merci, why do you keep sneaking up on me? You almost gave me a heart attack."

She doesn't say anything.

"Say something girl… what's wrong with you?"

"Hell, I'm in shock. Were you really talking to your mother like that and did you, for real, just hang up on her?" she laughs. "Girl, I bet she is grabbing her oil and on the way over here right now. Do you have a fever, are you sick or something? You're dying aren't you... how long do you have? Please Lord, not my sister!"

"Girl, stop playing," I say, slapping her hand from my face. "I'm fine, just tired of it all."

"I've been telling you to grow a backbone for a year but nooooo! Now that you've given them the power to control you it's going to be hard to snatch it from their grips. It's like an animal tasting the blood of their prey. However, listening to you just now, I do believe you are on the way chile!"

"Girl bye."

"Seriously Grayce, thank you for sticking up for me. I know that couldn't have been easy for you and I most definitely know that you have not heard the last of it. But I appreciate it."

"Yeah, yeah enough with all of this. How about you take your sister to lunch."

"Oh hell no, and have you throwing up over everything? No ma'am."

"Come on, I promise I won't."

Merci

"After lunch how about we do a little shopping? I have a date tonight and want to find something nice to wear," I say.

"A date with whoever it was that had you smiling so hard earlier?"

"Whatever nosey, but if you must know it's a guy I met a few weeks back at Bae Bae's Girls. He seems nice so we'll see what happens."

"The way you are blushing makes me think you like him a little," Grayce says, laughing.

"It's too early to tell but we did have a good time over breakfast that morning."

"Have you not seen him since?"

"No, he's been traveling with business but we've talked a lot and the conversations have been flowing easily, so hopefully our first dinner date will go even better. In spite of what you all think I would like to settle down eventually."

"I know, and it will happen if you stop judging all men by Daddy."

"Girl please! I am not thinking about your dried up daddy with his fake self. I'm waiting on God to send me who He has for me, but, in the meantime and in between time, I will continue to live this thang we call life."

Laughing, "Right on, sister girl! Are you ready to go so we can find you the perfect outfit for your date? Or better yet, since we have some time to kill, how about I treat you to a spa day?" Grayce suggests.

"You must really be sick and not telling me."

"Girl, come on!"

=====

We stop by Republic Coffee for a quick lunch and amazingly all of Grayce's food stays down, before trying this new spa I've been hearing great things about.

"Welcome to Blissful Spa, how can I help you?" the receptionist asks.

"We don't have an appointment but I was wondering if my sister and I can get a manicure, pedicure and massage?"

"Let me check," she says, tapping on the computer's keyboard. "Um, yes. We can get you both in. Would you like to get your massages first?"

"Sure, that will be great."

"Can I get your names?"

"I'm Grayce and this is my sister Merci."

"Alright ladies, follow me. Can I get you both something to drink? We have lemonade, water and wine."

"I'll take a glass of wine," I reply.

"Lemonade for me." Grayce says.

The receptionist shows us to the dressing area and we go in and change clothes.

I come out first and run smack into this guy who is also in a robe.

"Excuse me," I say, grabbing my robe that came open.

"No, excuse me," he says, smiling as he looks me up and down.

"Can I help you?" I ask, trying to get him to look at my face.

"Oh, I am so sorry, you look so familiar. Have we met?"

"No, we haven't."

"Are you sure? Hmm, you smell good," he whispers in my ear.

"Darrick?" Grayce says from behind me.

He pushes away from me. "Uh, hey, Grayce?" he says, looking at her.

"What are you doing here?" she asks.

"I'm here for a massage. What about you?"

"I'm here with my sister for a massage as well."

"Oh, is this, um, is this your sister?"

"Yes. This is my sister, Merci. Merci, this is Pastor Darrick Blair. He's Shaun's father and also a member at the church."

"Oh, I'm sorry to hear that," I say to him before taking a seat.

"Grayce, I had no idea you had a sister. Are you twins? Your parents never talk about her."

"No, we aren't twins but it was good seeing you, Pastor Blair, enjoy your massage."

Grayce

After two hours of pampering, we're finally dressed and preparing to leave the spa.

"Did you ladies enjoy your afternoon?" the receptionist asks.

"Yes, everything was great. What's our total?" Merci asks.

I move her out the way. "Don't you dare try to pay, I told you this was my treat."

"Actually, your bill has been paid by the gentleman who just left."

I look at Merci.

"Don't look at me. Obviously he likes one of us and I don't think it's me."

"What are you talking about? That's Shaun's dad."

"Yea, ok."

Looking back at the receptionist, I say, "Let me at least leave a tip."

"He took care of that as well. You ladies have an amazing evening."

Getting to the car, I can see Merci looking upside my head.

"What?" I ask.

"I haven't said anything."

"You didn't have to, it's written all over your face. Spit it out."

"Ok, what's going on with you and ole dude?"

"Who?"

"Don't play games with me, Grayce. What's going on with you and the good reverend?"

"Nothing. I told you, he's Shaun's—"

"Bullshit and you know it. Spill it!"

"There's nothing going on with us, I promise."

"If that's the lie you want to stick to, fine!"

"It's not a lie," I say, blowing out a breath. "Can we go to the mall now?"

Merci doesn't reply, she just smiles at my lying ass.

We spend an hour in the mall before finally leaving. We make it home to find our parents parked in the driveway.

"Grayce, I'm telling you now, I am not up for their mess today," Merci says.

"I'll handle them. You go ahead and get ready for your date," I tell her, pulling into the garage.

My sister gets out and doesn't even wait for them to get out the car, leaving me on my own.

Please God, don't let me get sick right now.

"Hey, what are you guys doing here?"

"We were on our way home and decided to stop and check on you because you were sick."

"I am not a child, you don't have to keep checking on me. I told you I was fine when I talked to you earlier."

"See what I mean?" my mother says. "She is starting to sound like Merci."

"No, I am not, and if you two came here for that you can get right back in your car and leave."

My mom doesn't say anything as she turns and heads back to the car.

"Look, little girl, I don't know what in the Sam hell has gotten into you but you'd better fix that smart mouth of yours. You're already starting to miss church and now disrespecting us. I won't stand for it. You'd better fix your attitude—"

"Or what, Daddy? Are you going to cut me off from the family like you've done Merci?"

"You know what, I am not about to have this conversation with you until you've come to your senses. Call me when that's done and I hope it's before bible study tomorrow night."

He turns to walk off before I even get a chance to answer.

Shrugging my shoulders, I get my bags out the car, let the garage door down and head into the house.

Merci

Putting the final touches on my outfit, I am beginning to get nervous. It's not like I haven't been out on a date but I guess I am tired of all these boys and ready for a real, steady relationship.

Glancing down at my watch, I see that it's 6:15.

Putting on some lip gloss, I grab my clutch before walking out my room.

"Grayce, I'm about to go."

"Well, don't you look cute? That top goes great with those jeans and they match your shoes perfectly," she says from the stairs.

"I know, right," I say, spinning around. "You did a great job picking them out."

"I have some fashion sense," she laughs.

"You do. And Grayce, thank you for today. I really enjoyed myself."

"I did too. Now, go and have fun. Do you know what time you'll be in?"

"No, mother, but I have my key."

Rolling her eyes, I laugh as I head out.

=====

I pull in to the restaurant. Turning off the ignition, I check my lip gloss and teeth before getting out. *Relax Merci*

Walking in, I head towards the bar. He spots me before I see him and calls my name.

Acknowledging him, I walk over to where he's now standing.

"Hey, you look handsome tonight."

"And you are looking just as beautiful as I remember," he says, kissing me on the cheek.

I slide into the booth as he slides in across from me.

"Do you know what you want to drink?" he asks as the waitress comes to the table.

"I'll talk a mojito, please."

"And for you sir," she asks?

"I'll have a glass of red wine and an order of crab cakes, please."

"Coming right up."

"Merci, I apologize. I didn't even ask if you eat crab cakes before I ordered."

"You're fine, but yes, I do."

"Great," he replies, fumbling with the napkin.

"If it makes you feel any better, I am as nervous as you," I say.

"You sure don't look like it." He smiles.

"I hide it well. And while we are being honest, let me say this. I know this is our first official date but I don't want to waste your time and I don't want you to waste mine."

"You're married?" he asks, looking confused.

"No, it's nothing like that. I am not in a relationship and I don't have any children, but with that being said, I'm not looking for a one night stand, a sex buddy or a quick fling. I am almost thirty years old and I am ready to settle down."

He shifts in his seat.

"Calm down." I say laughing. "I'm not saying I'm ready to get married and have children tomorrow but I am at a point in my life where I don't have time for games. I'm looking for a relationship, a real relationship, and if that's not what you're looking for then let's just enjoy dinner tonight and be friends."

Clearing his throat, "Well," he says, sipping his water. "I must be honest as well. I've never had a woman lay it all on the table like this."

"I apolo—"

"Please don't apologize, I like it. You said exactly what I'm feeling. I'm looking for a meaningful relationship as well. Although, it is our first date, so I'd like to get to know you better."

"Please don't say that and I end up finding out you're married with five children."

Laughing, he tells me, "No, I am not married and I have no children either, remember?"

"Whew," I say, pretending to wipe sweat from my forehead. "We're off to a great start," I respond as the waitress places our drinks and appetizer on the table.

"Are you ready to order?"

"Sure, I'll have the, um, Szechuan salmon."

"And for you, sir?"

"I'll have the rib-eye steak, medium well with a loaded baked potato."

"Sure thing. I'll put this right in for you guys. My name is Alex if you need anything."

Once she leaves, Thomas grabs my hand. "Do you mind if I pray over the food?"

"Please."

When he closes his eyes, I smile while watching him pray.

"Father, bless this food and drink we are about to receive. Please remove all impurities and bless the hands that prepared it for the nourishment of our bodies. Amen."

"Amen," I reply.

"Now, Ms. Alexander, tell me about yourself."

I go over the basics of my life, leaving out my family drama. I do tell him about Grayce and how we are rebuilding our relationship. He tells me that he is thirty-two, a plastic surgeon working at Regional One Hospital who loves to travel.

Before long, we've spent almost two hours talking and eating.

"Are you in a hurry to get home?"

"No, what do you have in mind?"

"How about a late movie?"

"Sure, I'd like that."

Walking out to my car, he stops. "Would you like to ride in the same car or is it too soon for that?"

"You aren't a serial killer or anything, are you?"

"I used to be but now I'm delivered," he says, trying to contain his laughter.

"Very funny. Come on, and I hope you like scary movies," I tell him, smacking him on the arm with my purse.

"Thank you for a great time tonight. I've really enjoyed myself."

"No, thank you for spending your Monday night with me. Let me get the door for you."

As he walks around the front of the car, I silently pray that this man is not playing with my heart.

"Madam," he says, holding his hand out.

"Thank you."

Walking to my car door, I turn and he's right behind me. Before I can even say anything he kisses me, deep and passionate.

When he releases me, he says, "I've wanted to do that all night."

Opening my car door, I can't say anything; all I can do is smile.

Getting inside, he leans in and kisses me again. "Call me when you make it home."

"I will."

Be still my heart. Whew!

Grayce

"Get up, you have to go before my sister gets home."

Grunting, he stirs but doesn't move.

"Come on, you have to get up."

"What time is it?" he asks, sitting up.

"It's almost one. Now, get up before she comes."

"Shit! I didn't know it was this late. Why didn't you wake me?"

"I've been trying for the last hour. COME ON!"

"Ok, dang! You'd think you were sixteen with the way you're acting."

"Oh, so you'll be ok with my sister seeing you in my bed?"

"No, but she won't see me unless she comes up here."

"What about your car?"

"It's down the street."

"It doesn't matter, I don't want to take the chance."

I throw him his shirt as I tie my robe around me. I am nervously pacing as he is slowly getting dressed. When he finally has his shoes on, I open the door to find Merci standing there with her hand up ready to knock.

"Merci? When did you get home?" I ask her, stuttering.

"Just now. I—" She stops mid-sentence when she looks behind me. "Pastor Darrick?"

"Um, I can explain," I say to her.

"You don't owe me an explanation, you're a grown woman. I only came to check on you before I went to bed but from the looks of it, you are just fine. I will see you in the morning."

With that she turns and walks away.

"Damn it!"

After letting Darrick out, I go to Merci's room.

"Merci." I tap on her door.

"Come in."

"Hey, I want to explain what you saw."

"Grayce, like I said before, you are grown and you don't owe me an explanation for the shit you do. However, I am feeling some type of way for you lying to me. I asked you point blank if anything was going on between the two of you and you looked me in the face and lied."

"I know and I'm sorry. I didn't know how to tell you. I mean, he is my ex-fiancé's father? How would that have looked?"

"Girl, when will you stop with the lies? You know damn well you and Shaun were never really engaged. He's as gay as they come."

"Fine! You're right but I don't know what to do, Merci."

"Sit down, Grayce," she says, moving the covers back on her bed.

"Is he the father of the baby?"

I don't say anything.

"Grayce?"

"It's possible."

"But?"

"But it's also possible he's not."

"Oh my God. You mean to tell me… Oh my God, Grayce."

I start to cry.

"Girl, what have I told your ass about crying? You weren't crying when you were getting knocked up. Besides, what in the hell is crying going to do?"

"I. DON'T. KNOW," I sob.

"Are you planning to keep the baby?"

"Yes."

"Then stop crying so we can figure this mess out. Shit! What do you want to do?"

Sniffling, I shrug my shoulders.

"Did you tell Darrick?"

"No, not until I figure everything out."

"Who is the other possibility? There is only one more, right?"

"Yes but—"

"But what? Who is it?"

"Warren."

"Warren who?"

"Uncle Warren."

"Wait, I hope Uncle is his first name and Warren is his last because surely you can't be talking about dad's ex-best friend."

I start crying again. This time a soul-stirring cry with runny nose and all.

"Bitch, have you lost your mind?" she asks, jumping up from the bed. "Out of all the dicks in Memphis, you happen to fall on Warren's? I know he's sexy but he's also the same age as your dad. Damn it Grayce!"

I'm still crying.

"Oh my freaking Lord! Your dad is going to kill you just as sure as your name. What in the hell were you thinking?"

I cry even harder.

"Yea, your ass better cry because when your dad finds out about this, there's going to be some slow singing and flower bringing."

"I'm so sorry!"

She goes into the bathroom and comes back with a towel. "Here, wipe your face child and stop crying before you make yourself sick."

"I don't know how I ended up here, Merci. My life is out of control. I'm pregnant and don't even know who the father is."

"Let me ask you a question, and please don't lie to me again. Did you sleep with Justice?"

"Why would you ask that?"

"Because I saw him a few weeks ago and he said something."

"What did he say?"

"He said to tell you he could still taste you in his mouth. Now answer the damn question."

"Yes."

"Is he a possibility for baby daddy?"

"No. I only slept with him once. I'm sorry, Merci."

"You've been sorry a lot. Damn! Didn't you have enough dick already or was doing him just something for you to do to have one up on me?"

"No! It was nothing like that."

"How can I believe you? All you seem to do is lie. I ought to slap the piss out of you just for breaking the girl code."

"I didn't think you had slept with him."

"That doesn't matter. You still violated. I don't know what else to say to you. What else have you lied about? You know what, don't even answer that. Just get out."

"Merci, please. I promise I didn't do that to hurt you. I saw Justice at the store one day and we started talking. He gave me his number and I took it, don't know why but I did. One night, I called him and we hooked up."

"The night you came in with your shirt on backwards?"

"Yea."

"And you call me a hoe? Wow."

"I'm sorry. I messed up."

"No ma'am, you're far past that but it's your life. And you have to figure out where to go from here."

I start crying again.

"You may as well stop those pitiful ass tears because I can bet you weren't crying then! Hell, crying won't fix your problem anyway and it's starting to work my nerves."

"I didn't mean to hurt you again?"

"You never do."

The next morning

We make it to the doctor's office for my appointment and I'm a nervous wreck.

"Grayce, stop shaking," Merci says, putting her hand on my leg.

"I can't help it. Talk so I won't have to think about why we are here. Tell me about your date last night."

"Dang it, Grayce. I never called Thomas when I got home last night. You and all that crying made me forget. He's probably thinking I didn't enjoy our date."

"Call him now."

"No, I'll send him a text real quick. Anyway," I continue, "It was great," I say smiling. "He seems like a great man and I hope he isn't with the shit."

"With the way you're smiling, I sure hope he isn't either. You need some happiness in your life because—"

"Grayce Alexander," the nurse calls.

"Saved by the bell. You coming with me?" I ask Merci.

"If you want."

"Please."

After stepping on the scale, peeing in a cup, answering what feels like one hundred questions and putting on a paper gown we are now waiting for the doctor to come in.

"Ms. Alexander?"

"Yes."

"I'm Dr. Mara Baker, what brings you in today?"

"Um, I went to Methodist Minor Medical Clinic a few days ago and I was told I'm pregnant."

"Ok, when was your last cycle?"

"They've always been spotty so I'm not absolutely sure."

"Ok," she says typing on her iPad. "Looking at the results on your urine test, you are definitely pregnant. We'll do an ultrasound to see how far along you are. Can you lie back for me? Is this your sister?"

"Yes."

"Would you like her to step out while I examine you?"

"No, it's fine. She can stay."

"Let me get my nurse and I'll be right back."

After coming back with the nurse, she proceeds to check me in all of my intimate places.

"You seem to be about twelve weeks judging by the size of your cervix but we will get an ultrasound just to be sure. Everything seems to be fine. Are you having any issues or do you have any questions?"

"Other than not being able to keep any food down."

"That's normal. It's called morning sickness, but as I am sure you are aware, it can happen at any time. It should go away within a few weeks seeing that you're almost into your second trimester. Anything else?"

"No, that's it."

"If you think of anything before you leave, please let me know. Otherwise, you can get dressed and I'll send you around to the imaging lab."

"Ms. Alexander, my name is Tanner and I'll be performing your ultrasound today. If you would lie back for me and raise your shirt."

After he turns off the light, he begins.

"Have you ever had an ultrasound before?"

"No."

"No problem," he says. "It won't hurt. I'm going to apply some jelly on your stomach and use this wand in order to see inside. It won't affect the baby at all. Now, if I'm able to tell the sex, would you like to know?"

I look over at Merci.

"Yes, we would," she replies, moving over to grab my hand.

He applies the jelly and begins. After a minute or so, I begin to hear a sound. "This is your baby's heartbeat; it's strong which is good. Hmm."

"Is everything alright?" Merci asks.

He doesn't say anything as he wipes off the wand and lies it down. "I'll be right back."

"Oh God, something's wrong," I say, beginning to panic.

"You don't know that. Stop jumping to conclusions."

"Why else would he leave like that?"

Just then, Dr. Baker comes in.

"Dr. Baker is everything alright?" I ask.

"Yes, I just want to check out something Tanner saw on the ultrasound. Relax for me, Ms. Alexander."

She applies more jelly before using the wand to look. After a minute, the sound of the baby's heartbeat fills the room again.

She smiles. Turning to me she says, "Congratulations, it looks like you're having twins."

"Twins! Are you sure?"

"Yes, look right here." She points to the screen. "This is Baby A and here's Baby B. You're actually fourteen weeks along. I'll calculate your due date in a moment."

I look over at Merci and her mouth is wide open.

"Twins? Oh my God. Merci, what in the hell am I going to do with twins?"

"Raise them."

"Would you like to know the babies' sex?"

"Yes, please!" she answers before I can.

"Well, Baby A is a girl and, um, Baby B is a boy. Let me check a few more things, print a few pictures for you then Tanner will get you cleaned up."

After a few more minutes, the lights are turned on and the doctor hands Merci the envelopes with the pictures of her niece and nephew.

"The babies are growing as expected. If all goes well, your due date will be October 7. Stop by the lab on your way out to have your blood drawn. Prescriptions for prenatal vitamins and iron pills will be up front when you check out. If there are no problems, I'll see you back in four weeks."

We walk out the room and Merci has the ultrasound pictures in her hand. I have my arm intertwined in hers as we head toward the lab.

"Grayce?"

We look up to see Warren.

"Uncle Warren."

"Are you pregnant?" he asks above a whisper before his wife Marie comes around the corner.

"Grayce! Merci!" she exclaims. "Oh my God! We haven't seen you girls in forever. Come and give your auntie a hug. How are you?"

"We're good, Marie. How are you?" Merci replies, stepping slowly as Marie reaches out to hug me.

"I am great. What are you guys doing here? Oh my God, you're pregnant?" Marie asks when she sees the pictures in her hand.

"Yes, I am," Merci answers, looking at me.

"Oh, that's great. Congratulations. How are your parents?"

"You'd have to ask Grayce."

"They're doing well. Dad is preparing to celebrate his anniversary at Emmanuel next month. You all should come."

"I don't know about that," Warren says, looking at me. "Give them our best. Come on Marie, you're going to be late for your appointment. It was good seeing you girls again."

"Merci, you didn't have to cover for me. Marie is nosey as hell and she's probably calling Dad right now."

"I thought they didn't speak anymore."

"He stopped talking to Warren, not Marie."

"What do you mean?"

"Nothing."

"Another family lie. Come on and get this blood drawn before she comes back."

"Are you sure you want to cover for me?"

"Girl, let me handle this. You're scared of Daddy, I'm not."

=====

By the time we make it home, our parents are already there.

"What are you doing here?" Merci asks with an attitude.

"Is it true? You're pregnant?" Dad asks through gritted teeth.

"What would make you think that, Dad?"

"Just answer the question."

"You have to answer one first: how did you find out? I know you haven't talked to Uncle Warren so—"

"How I found out is of no concern to you. So answer the question."

"If I am, what business is it of yours?"

Before she can continue, he slaps her. "You are a disgrace," he spits.

Without even hesitating, she slaps him back.

"Don't you ever put your filthy hands on me again! Now, get the hell off my property and don't ever come back."

When he doesn't move, she screams, "I mean it! Leave now or I'll have you in jail so quick it'll make your head spin."

"Grayce, get your stuff. You're coming home with me and your mother."

"Grayce Renee Alexander, you heard your father. Let's go."

"I'm not going anywhere," I say to them.

"What did you say?" my dad asks, walking towards me.

Merci steps in front of him. "Lay one finger on her and Mom will be burying you by Saturday."

"Grayce, if you stay here, consider yourself dead to me."

I open my mouth to respond but I feel myself getting sick so I bolt for the house.

"Grayce! Grayce, get back here!" he yells.

Merci closes the garage and leaves them standing there.

I come down the hall with a towel.

"You ok?" she asks.

"Yes, are you ok?"

"I'm good. It's going to take more than a slap from him to shake me."

Walking over to her, I hug her. "Thank you for having my back."

"That's what sisters do."

Merci

Doorbell rings...

"Hold on... I'm coming," calls Grayce. "Merci, are you expecting someone?"

"Yes," I scream from my bedroom.

"Who is it?" Grayce shouts to my closed door.

"Thomas Harvey."

Opening the door, he says, "Hey, I'm Thomas Harvey and I'm here to pick up Merci."

"Well, hey Mr. Harvey, please come in. I'm Grayce, Merci's sister. She should be out in a few minutes, can I offer you something to drink?"

"No thank you, I'm fine, and it's nice to finally meet you Grayce."

Have a seat and I'll go see what's keeping my sister."

Grayce hurries to my room. "Girlll, you didn't tell me Mr. Harvey was fine!" she laughs.

"I didn't? Hmm, it must have slipped my mind."

"Oh, I bet it did."

"Heifer, shut up! How do I look?"

"You look great, now hurry up and quit keeping that fine man waiting."

I don't take long to finish my makeup and hair before appearing before him in the den.

"Good evening Mr. Harvey, my apologies for keeping you waiting."

"Ms. Alexander if this is what I get for waiting please take your time. You look beautiful." he replies, looking me up and down.

"Flattery will get you everywhere, sir. Let's go."

Walking into Seasons 52, there is a line of people waiting. Looking around, I am impressed with the décor. "Have you been here before?" I ask.

"No but I've heard good things about it so I figured why not treat a beautiful lady to a great dinner at a nice restaurant."

"Keep on with the flattery and I may just keep you," I say, smiling at him.

"Hmm, I may take you up on that." He smiles back. "I'll go check on our reservation if you want to wait here."

The sitting areas are full so I lean against the wall and take out my phone to text Grayce.

"So, is that the guy who knocked you up?"

I stop midway through my text and look up into the face of my sperm donor. Rolling my eyes and taking a breath before answering, I reply, "My life is none of your business. In case you forgot, I stopped being your concern at seventeen."

"When you are out here in my city ruining my reputation, you make it my business," he says, raising his voice.

"Your reputation means nothing to me and the last time I checked, Memphis didn't belong to you, so if you'd kindly leave me the hell alone," I say, also raising my voice.

"Babe, are you ok?" Thomas asks as he walks up, putting his arm around me.

"Yes, I'm fine. My father was just leaving. Don't you have bible study tonight or, better yet, someone else's business to be in?"

"You must be the father of her bastard child?" he accuses Thomas.

Thomas looks at me and I get ready to reply but instead he continues, "Yes, I am. The name is Dr. Thomas Harvey, it's a pleasure to meet you sir," he says extending his hand.

"Doctor huh? I wonder how she trapped you." Daddy smugly asks. "You know she's nothing but a whore."

"You know what—"

"No babe, let me answer," Thomas says, cutting me off. "If you must know, pastor, is it?" Before he can answer Thomas continues, "Pastor Alexander, she didn't trap me, I trapped her. See, when I first laid eyes on this gorgeous brown-skinned beauty, I knew she would be my wife and I did everything possible until she said 'yes'."

My father's eyes widen. "Wife? If you're married, why is it I've never seen you around?"

"It's because you haven't looked hard enough. Now, let me make this perfectly clear so there won't be any misunderstandings from this point on: if you ever disrespect my wife again, I'll make sure you regret it." Grabbing my hand, he says, "Babe, let's eat somewhere else, I no longer like the atmosphere here."

I don't even look back as we walk out heading to the car.

After opening the door for me, he gets into the car. I have my head resting on the back of the seat because I've never been more embarrassed in my life.

Clearing his throat, he says, "Um, Mrs. Harvey, would you like to tell me about our baby?"

"I'm not pregnant, Grayce is. We found out a few days ago, and when we were leaving the ultrasound today, we ran into my uncle and his wife. Well, he's not really my uncle; he and my dad were best friends some years ago."

"Babe, slow down."

"I'm sorry. My dad gets on my nerves," I say, taking a breath. "Anyway, they saw the sonogram pictures in my hand so I told them I was the one pregnant to keep all of this from happening."

"So you took the blame for Grayce who is a grown woman?"

"Yea. It's a lot to explain and I don't know why I did it. I guess I thought I could handle our parents better than she could until she figures out what she wants to do. She's been under their thumb for as long as I can remember and she is scared of what they will do when they find out. I didn't know what else to do but protect her."

"I can understand that, but what is she going to do when it can no longer be hidden?"

"I don't know."

"I hope you don't mind me asking but what is the relationship between you and your dad?"

"To be honest, we haven't had one since I was about fourteen. I don't know why. All I know is, something changed and he's hated me ever since. He would blame me for anything that happened. If a glass broke, he had a bad day, tithes were down at the church or whatever, I was the reason. And Grayce, she could do no wrong and she knew it. So she'd do whatever she wanted because I'd get in trouble for it. I put up with it for as long as I could and that was at seventeen. I left and never looked back."

"I'm sorry. I didn't mean to pry into your family business."

"It's a little too late for that, seeing that you're my husband, remember?" I say with a smile which causes him to laugh. "You know, my dad used to be a hero in my eyes and I didn't think there would be anything he could do to make me hate him, but man was I wrong. One evening he comes home and sees a boy running from our bedroom window and, just like all the times before, he blamed me."

"What happened?"

"He beat—" I clear my throat to avoid crying. "He beat the hell out of me. I'd never seen him like that before. He treated me like I was nothing to him, leaving me naked, bruised and bleeding on the kitchen floor of our house. It didn't matter what I said, his mind was made up. After that, I left his house and never went back. Needless to say, I really hadn't seen any of them until about a year ago when Grayce showed up on my doorstep. I don't even know why I let her stay but I did."

"Babe, I am so sorry. How did you manage all by yourself at seventeen?"

"It was nothing but God's grace. I'd be lying if I said it was anything else because I never wanted for anything. Yes, there were times I missed having a family to share the holidays with but I made it through and I was determined to never be treated that way by anybody else."

Thomas just looks at me and smiles.

"Why are you looking at me like that?" I ask.

"I am in awe of how strong you are."

"Yea right! I wouldn't blame you if you wanted out right now," I say through tears.

"Come here," he says pulling me as close as he can across the console. "Merci, I really like you and if that means I have to put up with your family drama then so be it. I am a grown man, I can handle it, and one thing I will make sure of: your dad won't ever make you cry again."

After hearing those words, I cry harder.

"Now, if you're going to be a cry baby, I may have to rethink this," he replies before laughing.

"Hush, and kiss me."

After spending another twenty minutes in the car, we settle on eating at The Waffle House. *I know, right.* But it ends up being just as great as our first date. We sit and talk for hours, over waffles and coffee.

Grayce

Watching a movie on the couch, I hear my cell phone vibrating on the table. I pick it up and see that it's Warren. I press ignore but he calls again.

"Hello," I answer, agitated.

"Is your sister home?"

"No, why?"

"Open the door, I need to talk to you."

"There's nothing to talk about, Warren, go home."

"Grayce, open the door."

I end the call and wait a minute before opening the door.

"What do you want?" I ask as he comes rushing in.

"Are you pregnant?"

"What?"

"You heard me. ARE. YOU. PREGNANT?"

"I TOLD YOU NO!" I scream back.

"I don't believe you. Just tell me the truth so that we can deal with this mess properly before anyone gets hurt."

"Who could possibly get hurt if I were pregnant? I'm not understanding."

"You, me, our families. Do you know what would happen if your father finds out you're having my baby?"

"No, because I'm not pregnant."

"Stop lying. Damn it!"

I look at him after his tone gets very aggressive. "Look, it's time for you to go."

Forcefully grabbing my arm, he says, "I don't have time for your childish ass games. Tell me the truth: are you pregnant with my baby?"

"Let me go! Who in the hell do you think you are?"

Releasing my arm, he looks at me with an anger I've never seen.

"I'm someone you don't want to mess with, little girl."

I laugh. "Oh wow, so I'm a little girl now? Was I a little girl when you had your face buried in my ass? Now you got the nerve to stand in my house threatening me with this macho man routine because you're afraid of my daddy? Man, get your ass on. I don't have to explain anything to you nor my daddy. I'm very grown."

He walks closer, grabbing me by the neck. "Don't fuck with me, Grayce! I will make your life a living hell!" he screams.

"Warren, stop!" I say, trying to pry his hand from my neck.

He releases me and I slide to the floor. I don't know why until I see Merci standing there with the remnants of a lamp in her hand.

"Grayce, are you ok?" she asks, kneeling down next to me.

"Yea, I'll be fine."

"I'm calling for an ambulance."

"NO!"

"What do you mean, no? You need to get checked out," she says as Thomas comes charging into the house.

"Merci! What the hell?" he asks when he sees Warren on the floor. "What happened?"

"I caught him choking Grayce."

"Dude, are you ok?" Thomas asks Warren as he starts to get up.

"Yea, get your hands off of me," Warren snaps.

"I'm just trying to help," Thomas says stepping back.

"I don't need your help," he shouts while staggering to stand.

"Well then, stagger your dumb ass to your car and leave my house before I have you arrested," Merci says.

"I'm not going anywhere until Grayce tells me what I need to know."

"Look dude, take your ass on out of here before that cut on the back of your head is the least of your worries," Thomas says.

"I'm not going anywhere, I told you that!"

Thomas grabs Warren by the arm and slings him out the door. "Go get your head looked at, man, and don't come back here."

"Grayce, what in the hell is going on?" Merci asks once the door is closed.

"We will talk about it later. I'm going upstairs. You two enjoy the rest of your night."

"Are you serious? I come in to find Warren's hands around your neck and you want me to worry about it in the morning? Get your ass back here."

"Merci, I don't want to argue with you, ok?"

"And I don't want to argue with you, but you need to tell me what the hell happened and you're going to do it now."

"I don't know what has gotten into him. He wanted me to admit that I was pregnant and when I didn't he got violent. Then you came in."

"Dammit, Grayce!"

Merci

"You need to go to the ER to have your neck checked out," I tell her.

"I'm fine."

"No, you're not. At least let Thomas look at it."

"I'm fine."

"Grayce!"

"Ok, but stop yelling."

Thomas looks at her neck and, after a few squeezes, he says she'll be a little bruised but otherwise alright.

"Now, can I go to bed, mother?" Grayce asks.

"I'm just worried about your ole funky ass."

"I know and I'm sorry. It just seems like everything is going wrong at the same time."

"I get that but don't take it out on me."

"I'm sorry, Merci."

"Go to bed. If you need me, let me know."

After Grayce goes upstairs, I clean up the mess from the lamp and make sure the front door is locked before joining Thomas on the couch.

"Are you sure you want to become a part of all this?" I ask, while grabbing the remote to turn the TV off.

"You can't get rid of me that easily."

"Alright but don't say I didn't warn you," I laugh.

He pulls me onto his lap. I look in his eyes before kissing him. Moaning into his mouth as his hands begin to roam under my dress, I become lost in him.

"You feel so good," he says, causing me to stop.

He looks at me.

"I'm sorry," I say before moving from his lap.

"What's wrong?"

"There's nothing wrong. It's just, I can't do this. I like you, a lot, and I don't want to ruin what we're building with sex. As bad as I want to take you into my bedroom right now, I can't. I'm sorry."

He doesn't say anything. He stands and fixes the noticeable erection in his pants. He then grabs my hand and pulls me up.

"You don't owe me an apology. As a matter of fact, I'm glad you stopped because I agree with you. I like you too, Merci, and I want to get to know you and your mind; I'll have plenty of time to get to know your body."

I look at him and smile. "You're not upset?"

"No," he says sitting us down on the couch. "Merci, I've been celibate for over a year now so waiting a while longer won't kill me."

"A year? Wow! You are a rare breed."

"I'm not rare, but I am a man who is tired of creating soul ties with women who aren't my soul mate. After my last relationship ended, I made a vow to God that I wouldn't have sex with another woman until I found my wife."

"What happened with your last relationship? If you don't mind me asking."

"We dated for almost two years but realized we were on different paths. Everything she wanted could be bought from a store whereas I was looking for something that only God could give. That's a Godly woman with a good heart, morals and wife standards."

"Ok, I hear that."

"What about you?"

"To be honest, I've never had a meaningful relationship. I think it was because of being so caught up in the hurt from my father. I allowed it to hinder me from opening up to anyone. And although I haven't had physical sex in a while, I have indulged in oral, which I am not proud of."

"You're human and entitled to make mistakes. Don't beat yourself over the head."

"I know, but it's like you said, creating soul ties which can be very hard to break."

"I totally understand. What's different now?"

"What do you mean?"

"Why are you ready to be in a relationship with me?"

"I think it had something to do with mending the relationship with Grayce. It was when I began to do that, I realized all the things I'd been missing out on. Plus, I'm getting older and ready for a husband to show me how a real man loves a woman. I don't know if that's you but I sure hope it is."

"I'm not perfect, Merci, but I've watched my dad love my mom for over forty years and I want a love like that. He has taught me everything I know and I will try my very best to never intentionally hurt you. All I ask is that you give me a chance to love the broken parts of you. I can't promise that I won't make some mistakes but I will do everything in my power to love the hurt out of you."

"How do you know that and we just met a month ago? Can you honestly say I'm the person you're supposed to be with?"

"Actually it's been forty-six days since I laid eyes on you but let me ask you this, are you a believer of God?"

"Yes."

"Do you believe He leads us to the one we're supposed to be with?"

"Without a doubt."

"Then you'll understand when I say I prayed for you. Merci, for the last year, through fasting and prayer, I've asked God to send me the woman who would complete me, not one that would compete with me. I prayed for a woman who can pray for me on the days I can't pray for myself. I prayed for a woman I can pray for on the days she can't pray for herself. And I specifically asked for a woman who knows whose she is because if she knows that, everything else will fall into place. I didn't have to give God a list of what was acceptable or not because I knew He'd have her made perfect for me. Believe this or not, that morning at the café when you walked in, I knew it was you."

"How could you possibly know that?"

"Because I'd never been to that café before. But that particular morning, I was led there. I didn't know why until you walked in. You are my rib, Merci Alexander, you are my favor and if you'll have me I will spend every day making sure you know that."

I start to cry.

"I don't know—"

He grabs my hands, cutting me off. Kneeling in front of me he begins to pray and I cry even harder...

"Our Father in Heaven, holy is your name oh God. I come praying to you first thanking you for another day. God I know everything that happens in our lives is ordained by you and I believe you leading me to this young lady was not by accident. I now ask that you cover us so that I can be the man you've designed me to be and Merci can be the woman you desire her to be. God, heal her mind, mend her broken pieces, create in her a clean heart and renew a right spirit within her to know she's made in your image. Lord, destroy the generational curses of anger and bitterness so they no longer have dominion and power over her. Allow the

walls of bondage to be torn down so that she will let love back in. Give me the strength to love her back to life. Show her your righteousness and love as she stops fighting what is meant for her. I praise and thank you God as I submit this prayer to you now. Amen."

He then pulls me into a hug.

"I've never had a man pray for me before."

"I'll always pray for you because that's what I'm supposed to do. I'm going to go. I have rounds at the hospital in the morning. I'd love to see you before you leave for New York on Monday."

"How about we go to church together Sunday?"

"I'd like that. I had a great time tonight, Mrs. Harvey."

"I did too, Mr. Harvey. Call me when you get home. I should be showered and in bed by then."

"Definitely. Lock up after me," he says before kissing me.

Closing the door, I lean against it for a minute before turning on the alarm and turning out the lights.

Getting to my bedroom, I do something I haven't done in a while. I kneel beside my bed and pray.

"Lord, please let this man be from you and made just for me. Amen."

Grayce

"Hey, I thought you'd be up by now. You want some coffee or some ginger tea?" Merci asks as I walk into the kitchen.

"Some ginger tea please," I reply, sitting at the table.

"How is your neck?"

"It's fine. There's only a few spots of bruising."

"You need to go and see Dr. Baker, just to make sure everything is alright. Are you still having morning sickness?"

"Yes and I hope it ends soon. I have to go back to work on Monday. The last thing I need is someone finding out."

"Girl, stop worrying about what people will think. It's time for you to live for Grayce and no one else."

"You're right but it's hard," I say as she sits the cup in front of me. "So how was your date last night?"

"He prayed for me," she says, sitting across from me.

"What?"

"Last night, he prayed for me. Like real deal prayed, right in front of me. Hand holding and eyes closed type praying."

"What did you do?"

"I cried like a baby," I admit, laughing. "Grayce, I've never had a man personally pray for me. Prey on me, yes but never pray for me. I'm not used to it."

"Do you like him?"

"Yes, a lot."

"Then what's the issue?"

"I've never had a real relationship. I don't want to mess it up and I damn sure don't want to mess this man up."

"Then don't. All you have to do is get out of your own way. Pray about it and let God lead you."

"Alright, Ms. Sunday school."

"I'm serious."

"I know, and I am too. I really want this to work."

"Are you seeing him before you leave for New York?"

"Yes, we're going to church together in the morning."

"Hmm, he sounds like a keeper."

"I'm starting to believe that. Oh, girl with everything happening last night, I forgot to tell you who we ran into."

"Oh Lord! Who?"

"Your daddy."

"Shut up! Where?" she laughs.

"At the restaurant. He was ranting and raving, talking about I must have trapped Thomas by getting pregnant."

"Are you serious? Oh my God, what did you say?"

"I didn't have to say anything, chile, Thomas handled it. Told daddy we were married and he was the father of my baby."

I spit my tea out. "You lying!"

"I was standing there with my mouth open while Thomas tore him a new one. Then he grabbed my hand and walked out."

"And left Daddy standing there? I wish I could have been there," I laugh.

"It's funny now but I was so embarrassed. I just don't understand why he hates me so much. What did I ever do to him?"

"I don't know, and we aren't going to ruin our day trying to figure out Pastor Alexander. And you aren't going to allow his issues to ruin this for you. Thomas seems like a good man. Build on that and not from the foolish things of Daddy."

"I hear you and I won't. I will no longer live in that shadow. Now, not to change the subject but what are you going to do about your two situations?"

"I don't know, Merci."

"Are you keeping them?"

"Yes, I'm definitely sure of that."

"But?"

"It's a mess. I don't even know who the father is."

"That can be easily resolved with a DNA test. What else? Please don't tell me you're worried about what Dad and Mom will say."

"No, well yes, a little."

"Grayce!"

"I can't help it. Then I have Warren to worry about. I've never seen him like that before. From the anger in his eyes last night, he's more afraid of Daddy than his own wife."

"Well, that's his problem, not yours. The only thing you need to worry about is the health of those two babies in your belly."

"I know, and I am," I say as Merci's phone rings. "Go ahead and answer your phone. I'm going to get dressed. I have some errands to run."

Pressing answer on her phone, she covers it, "Do you need me to go with you?"

"No, I won't be out long."

=====

Walking out to my car, I see a black rose and a card. Looking around, I pick up the card and open it.

'SO YOU LIKE SLEEPING WITH MARRIED MEN! I WONDER WHAT DADDY WOULD SAY?'

Before I can even get into the car good, my cellphone rings with an unknown number.

"Hello?"

"I see you liked my gift."

"Who is this?"

"You'll find out soon enough."

The call disconnects. A few seconds later, it rings again.

"WHO IS THIS?" I scream.

"Uh, Ms. Alexander, this is Bill from Payne's Renewal."

"Oh Bill, I am so sorry."

"It's no problem. I was calling to see if you were still interested in the house you looked at because I have another potential renter."

"I haven't even had time to really think about it. Go ahead and rent it, and if I still need a place, I'll give you a call."

"Sure thing. I look forward to hearing from you."

Finally getting in the car, I try to think of who could have left me this card. I couldn't recognize the voice because it was muffled. I pull to the end of the driveway and put the rose and the card in the garbage can. I don't need Merci finding it.

Whoever it is, I'll deal with it but for now, I have other things to do.

I head to the bank to fill out some paperwork, adding Merci to all of my accounts. I also add her as beneficiary to the life insurance I have through them. I haven't told her I'm making any of these changes but being pregnant, I want to make sure she's capable of handling all of my affairs in case something happens.

On the way home, I stop by Motherhood Maternity to get a few pairs of pants and some dresses because it seems as if I am getting bigger overnight. At least with some baggier clothes, I can mask this stomach a little while longer.

Walking out the store, I run right into Marie, Warren's wife.

"Grayce, is that you?"

Rolling my eyes, "Yes Marie."

"What are you doing at a maternity store?"

"Shopping. What are you doing here?"

"I was actually about to meet my husband for lunch at Ruth Chris next door, care to join us?" she says as Warren walks up.

Seeing me, he instantly frowns.

"Warren, look who it is."

"Oh yea, hi Grayce."

"Warren," I reply.

"I was asking her if she wanted to join us for lunch. Maybe you can convince her," she says, looking at him.

"Uh, it looks like she's busy. Maybe some other time."

"He's right. I have some more errands to run. Maybe another time."

Merci

"Thank you so much," I say to the courier who delivers the files I need for my New York trip. They were supposed to be here a few days ago but with everything going on, I hadn't even thought about them.

I take the files and head into my office. Spreading them out on the desk, a USB drive drops out. I power on my laptop and begin to go through the many documents. I send a message to Mrs. Glassor letting her know I've received the files and that I will take care of everything.

Once I hit send, I plug in the USB and double click on the encrypted file. It asks for a password. Flipping through the assorted papers, I finally find it and type it in. It opens up a file of employees suspected of being the embezzler. Mrs. Glassor has made sure that I have a copy of each of their personal files. I start to read through a few of them, making a few notes.

I continue flipping through them until I hear the alarm sound.

"Hey," Grayce says, standing in the door.

"Hey, where have you been?"

"I had some things to take care of. I also went to pick up some maternity clothes and you'll never guess who I ran into?"

"Please don't say Warren."

"Worse, his wife."

"Was she still fishing for information?"

"Of course, but there's something else I need to tell you."

"Oh Lord, not another baby daddy," I say putting my head in my hands.

"No, but this morning, I found a card and a rose on my car window."

"Ooo-k. Who left it?"

"I don't know but whoever it is knows I've been sleeping with a married man."

"Oh wait, it was a stalker type card?"

"Yea."

"Why didn't you tell me this morning?"

"I wasn't going to tell you at all but I got a phone call right afterwards and it was like whoever left it was watching me."

"Do you know who it was?"

"No, they had their voice masked."

"That's it, I'm going to cancel my trip."

"No! Don't do that."

"Grayce, there is no way I am going to leave you here by yourself when someone is stalking you."

"We don't know that for sure. It could be Warren trying to scare me."

"Well, if you aren't scared, I am. Why don't you come to New York with me? You can hang out while I work."

"I wish I could but I need to get back to work."

"At least come for a few days. Use some of those vacation days you have saved."

"I'll think about it."

"I'm serious, Grayce."

"I will. Now, why don't you order a pizza while I take a shower because I am starving?"

"Yes ma'am."

When she leaves, I call the home security company I use and ask them about installing some cameras as well as some motion lights around the house. They can't fit me in for another few weeks. I don't want to leave her here alone but I have to go to New York. Maybe I can get Thomas to check in on her while I'm gone.

Grayce

Sounds of someone beating on the door.

I roll over and look at the clock on the nightstand. *Who in the hell is beating on the door at 5:30 in the morning.*

Merci is already in New York so I get up to look out the window but I don't see a car.

More pounding.

I put on my robe and grab my cell phone. Punching in 911, I wait to press call. Walking down the stairs, I scream "Who is it?" but no one responds.

"Who is it?" I scream again and still nothing.

They pound on the door again causing me to jump.

"If you don't identify yourself, I'm calling the police."

They continue to pound. I press call.

"911, what is your emergency?"

"Someone is trying to break into my home."

"Ma'am, what is your address?"

"7125 Stone Field Road, Olive Branch, MS."

"I'm dispatching a unit to you right now, stay on the line."

Just then, something is thrown through the window, setting off the alarm.

"Oh my God, they just threw something through the window."

"Help is on the way."

"Please hurry."

After a few minutes, I see the flashing lights. I let the dispatcher know before releasing the call.

I run over to turn off the alarm before opening the door.

"Ma'am, are you alright?" the officer asks, stepping onto the porch with his weapon drawn.

"Yes. Whoever it was threw something through the window."

"Do you give me permission to enter your home?"

"Yes, please."

We walk over to the item that is inside the living room. I reach to grab it.

"No, don't touch it," he warns. "Let me get some gloves from my car."

He walks out as my cell phone begins to vibrate. *Shit!*

"Grayce, are you okay? Why was the alarm going off?"

"How did you know the alarm was going off?"

"I have an app on my phone that alerts me but that isn't the point, what's wrong?"

"I'm fine. Someone was beating on the door."

"Who?"

"I don't know. The police are here now."

"The police. Oh God, I'm coming home."

"No, don't do that. Everything is going to be fine. I'll call you once they leave."

"Don't forget, or else I'll be on the next plane."

When the officer comes back, he begins to open the object. It's a bloodied doll with a knife sticking out. There is a note that says, 'You're next.'

"Oh my God!"

"Ma'am, do you have any idea who would do something like this?"

"No! I've been receiving some notes and calls but I don't know who they are from."

"I'm going to have our crime scene unit come out to collect this as well as try to get some prints from the door. Is there anywhere else you can stay tonight?"

"Yes, I'll go to a hotel."

"Why don't you go ahead and pack a bag. This window will also need to be covered."

"Thanks, I'll see about calling someone."

I go upstairs and slip into some sweats, a t-shirt and tennis shoes. I throw a few things in a bag before heading back downstairs. I go into Merci's office to use her computer while waiting on the crime scene unit to show up.

I search and find a company with an after-hours number who can come and board the window. Just then my phone rings again.

"Merci, I'm alright."

"Are you sure? What is the police saying?"

"We are waiting on crime scene—"

"Crime scene!"

"Calm down. It's only to get some prints off the door."

"Grayce, is that it? Are you really okay?"

"Yes. The officer suggested I stay at a hotel tonight so that's what I'm going to do."

"Man, I don't like that you're there alone."

"I can take care of myself."

"I know but I'm still worried."

"You don't have to worry, I'm a big girl."

"Yes, but you're no match for a stalker, Grayce."

"I will be fine and I will call you if I need you. I'm sorry I woke you, I know you have a busy day."

"You didn't, I was already up, but don't forget to call me if you need me."

"I won't, I promise."

"I mean it, Grayce."

I hang up the call and put my head in my hands. I don't know how I got to this point in my life. I didn't even tell Merci about the doll because I know she'd come home and I couldn't do that knowing she has a job to do. I'll find a way to deal with this mess on my own.

After a few hours, the window is patched up with the guy coming back tomorrow to replace the glass. I lock up and head to a hotel.

Another day of missed work.

Next day

I am finally headed back to work. Getting to the school, I head to my classroom to get things situated before the students arrive. I go into the teacher's lounge to fix some tea in the hopes of keeping this nausea under control.

As the first bell rings, the children come storming down the hall.

"Ms. Alexander, Ms. Alexander, we're so glad you're back."

"I'm glad to be back. Have you all been behaving?" I ask my third grade class.

"Yes ma'am," they all say in unison.

"Good. Go ahead and put your backpacks away and get out your notebooks for bell work."

I look around at the many faces and smile. I love being a teacher. It's something I've wanted to be since I was a child.

After a few hours, the children are at recess with my teacher's assistant and I am preparing to eat my lunch when Joann from the office calls on the intercom.

"Grayce, you have a delivery in the office. Do you want me to have it sent down?"

"No, I'll get it before I leave."

"Ok. And we are glad to have you back. We missed you."

"Thanks Joann. I missed you guys too."

Two weeks later - Merci

May

I've been in New York two weeks working this embezzlement case, and although I've been making some progress, I am anxious to get home. I've been worried sick about Grayce and this stalker she has. She keeps telling me that she's alright but I know she's lying. Knowing her, it's probably getting worse. She did tell me about some notes that were sent to her job and a call to her principal to get her fired.

The security company still haven't installed the cameras I asked for, and when I called today they promised me they would be out first thing tomorrow morning.

Thomas has been a great help by checking on her but she threatened bodily harm if he didn't leave her alone. So now I am back to worrying. Yes, it's a big mess yet the police aren't any closer to finding out who it is. I did talk to Grayce today and she sounded good, probably to keep me from asking questions. She said there were no signs of the stalker today and she'd finally stopped having morning sickness.

"Ms. Alexander, Agent Oliver Benton is here from the NYPD Special Fraud Unit," Carolina, the receptionist, says snapping me out of my thoughts.

"Send him in."

I get up and open the door as he turns the corner to my office.

"Agent Benton, it's good seeing you again. Please tell me you have some good news."

"As a matter of fact, I do. I heard from my team and we were finally able to break into the encrypted files you located on the company's servers."

"That's great. Are you any closer to identifying the person because I am about sick of going through all this paperwork and I'm ready to get home?"

"I understand that and yes, we were able to track the last deposit to a bank account that, if you looked on paper, seemed like a legitimate business but it was all fraudulent. My team was able to do some digging and it all came back to Landon McGuire."

"That bitch! I knew she had something to do with this but I needed to be sure. Judging by her lifestyle, there's no way she could afford all that she has on her salary."

I look at Det. Benton and he seems lost in thought. "Detective, is there more? You seem flustered."

"I don't know any other way to say this but straight out. I know her."

"Her who? Landon?"

"Yes."

"How?"

"We've been on a few dates."

"Are you kidding me? How did you all meet?"

"I wish I was. I meet her about six months ago at a coffee shop not far from my office."

"Wow, okay. Is it serious?"

"I honestly thought it was but now I'm starting to think she played me."

"How so?"

"I've been replaying our last few dates. She always wanted to discuss my job, asking questions that made me believe she wanted to get to know more about me but now I know she was just trying to cover her tracks."

"Well, I can give her credit because she's done a damn good job. I'm grateful she was greedy enough to try it again. Because, had it not been for the extra security measure installed a few weeks ago, we probably would have never found out who it was."

"Wow, she used me," he says.

"You probably weren't the first because she's been pulling this scheme for over three years and my calculation shows she's gotten away with almost three million dollars. Which is why it doesn't make sense for her to still be here, working. She has plenty of money to start over somewhere else."

"She'd gotten comfortable in her wrong and stopped thinking she could get caught. I see it all the time. From what we can tell, she was unaware of that extra security added to the system and it left her marks all over this last transaction."

"Nobody knew about the upgrade except me and the owner. Before I got here, she had a second layer of security added that captured the user ID of anyone moving money."

"It's a good thing she did. I just cannot believe I let my guard down. Unfreakingbelieveable! Is she here today?" Detective Benton asks.

"Of course, she just got back from a fourteen-day vacation that she's been bragging about. Let me get our head of security to come down before I call her. Carolina?"

"Yes Ms. Alexander."

"Can you please page Paul from security and have him meet me in my office."

"Sure thing."

Detective Benton gets up and starts pacing. "I just cannot believe this. She's been lying to me this entire time."

"You know, my grandmother says that a lie doesn't care who tells it."

Just then there is a knock on the door.

"Ms. Alexander, you wanted to see me?" Paul says, sticking his head in.

"Yes, come in. Agent Benton, this is Paul Malone, head of security."

"Nice to meet you," Paul says, extending his hand.

"Have a seat," I tell Paul.

"Anything wrong?" he asks, looking concerned.

"Paul, for the last two weeks, I've been working on a case of embezzlement here in the company."

"Embezzlement? From Ms. Glassor? Do you know who is it?"

"Yes, I was just informed by Detective Benton of the identity of the suspect: it's Landon McGuire."

"Head of accounting Landon?"

"That's the one."

"I'm not shocked."

"Why do you say that, Paul?"

"She's too cocky and always bragging. What happens now?"

"We arrest her," Benton says.

"Do you need me to go and get her?" he asks, jumping up from the chair.

I laugh. "No, I'm going to have Carolina send her in."

"You sure? It would do me a great pleasure to be the one to walk her out."

"You can get that pleasure just as soon as I break the news to her."

Laughing, I buzz Carolina and ask her to have Landon stop by my office. Before I can respond to the guys, my cell phone vibrates. I look and see that it's Grayce so I send her a message letting her know I'm in a meeting and will call her back.

"Detective, is there a certain way you want to—" Before I can even finish my sentence, the door swings open.

"What can I do for you? I was in the middle—"

She stops when she sees who is in my office.

"What is this? Oliver, what are you doing here?" She smiles. "What's going on?"

"Landon, would you have a seat. There's something we need to discuss."

Det. Benton and Paul move to the side of my desk.

"Ok," she says with a wide grin. "What's up? Do yawl have a surprise for me or something?"

"You can say that."

"What is it? Oliver, babe, what's going on?"

"I'll let Ms. Alexander explain."

"Okay," she says turning to me and no longer smiling.

"Landon, for the last two weeks I've been on a special assignment from Ms. Glassor."

"What kind of special assignment?"

"She sent me here to investigate possible acts of embezzlement."

"Ok. So, why am I here? What in the hell does that have to do with me?"

"I'm glad you asked. Det. Benton and I, along with his team at NYPD, have been working together to find out who is behind it."

"You never told me that," she says to Det. Benton through gritted teeth.

"And up until today, we had a hard time figuring out who the culprit was."

"I ask again, what in the hell does this have to do with me?"

"Everything, in fact. See, the person committing the crime had become good, great in fact, at covering their tracks. However, what they didn't know was that a second tracker was embedded into the system to capture the ID of anyone moving money from one account to another."

Her face starts turning fire red.

"Do you know what that means, Ms. McGuire?"

"No."

"That means that your ass is busted." Paul belts out.

I look at him trying not to laugh. "Landon, how could you steal from the one person who trusted you? Mrs. Glassor gave you a chance when no one else would. And now for you to steal from her? You should be ashamed."

"That's a lie!" she shouts, jumping to her feet. "That's a bald face lie! I've never stolen anything from this company."

Det. Benton walks forward with a folder which he lays in front of her. "Take a look."

"I will not!"

"Look at the damn folder," he says, raising his voice. "All the evidence you need is right in front of you."

Without opening it, she moves in front of him. "Oliver, why are you doing this to me? You know I'd never do anything like this."

"No, all I know is that you're a user, liar and manipulator. Tell me this: was what we had a part of your sick game?"

"No! Baby, you've got to believe me. They are setting me up."

"Cut the bullshit and put your hands behind your back."

"Are you seriously going to arrest me?"

"Yes, I am."

"Fuck you, Oliver!" she yells.

As he tries to grab her arm, she starts swinging and cursing. Paul has to restrain her in order to finally get the cuffs on. By the time they open my office door there is a crowd of employees trying to figure out what's going on.

Landon is taken out of the office kicking and screaming and Paul has the privilege of walking her out. I advise Agent Benson that I will meet him downtown to sign the paperwork needed to officially file charges against her.

=====

After many hours and a multitude of paperwork later, Landon is safely tucked in at the city jail. I've already spoken to Mrs. Glassor and filled her in on everything. She is happy to have this mess finally figured out. I tell her it'll be a few months before the Attorney General finalizes the case against Landon, and a few more months before we'd have to come back to testify.

I order a bottle of wine from room service to celebrate. Finishing a second glass, I pack my bags and lay out my clothes for the flight home tomorrow. Preparing to shower, I remember that I didn't call Grayce back. I grab my phone and dial her number but she doesn't answer.

I'll call her again before I go to bed.

Grayce

Today has been great. I had a doctor's appointment and all is well with the babies. I've finally stopped having morning sickness which means I am eating like crazy. I guess this is why I've gained seven pounds but Dr. Baker said weight gain is sometimes a little more than normal when expecting multiples. Whew, I've got to get this together before I end up gaining fifty pounds.

Anyway, it's been a week since I've had any run-ins with this stalker. *Thank you, Jesus.* I hope whoever it was is done. It was starting to get crazier. I haven't even told Merci everything because I didn't want her to worry while in New York. Although the last stunt, a car seat on the doorstep with a note saying, 'Time's up', was the scariest; I couldn't tell her. I didn't know what it meant and I wasn't going to worry about it.

I initially thought it was Warren's wife but I talked to him today and he swears it's not because she's traveling. I took all the items to the police station and even though they promise to work on figuring out who it is, I don't think they are taking it serious.

Nevertheless, since there hasn't been anything lately, I'm not about to spend the rest of my good day worrying over it.

I get up and double check the locks on the doors and make sure the alarm is on because I have a funny feeling. Almost like I'm being watched. I shake it off, take a shower, put on a huge t-shirt and prepare to relax with a movie.

I go into Merci's office. I don't know why, but for some reason I feel the need to write her a letter. I turn to leave and the feeling gets stronger so I sit at her desk, grab a notepad and pen. Before I begin, I pray to God.

God, if this is you, please guide my pen and my thoughts. Amen.

I jot down some extra thoughts on a separate piece of paper and place it in her desk drawer before starting the letter.

After finishing, I wipe the falling tears before placing the letter in an envelope and laying it on her bed. Walking back down the hall, I hear something in the kitchen. Merci had me download the security app on my phone and when I pull it up, it shows the alarm is still armed so I continue walking.

Turning into the kitchen...

"Shit! How did you get in here?"

"It was easy."

"Have you been here this entire time?"

"Yes."

"How? Why? What do you want?"

"I can see you didn't take my advice."

"What advice was that?"

"The note, the doll, the car seat; don't you remember?"

"That was you?"

"Of course, who else would it have been? Oh, let me guess, you have another baby daddy besides my husband." She laughs. "I knew you were a whore."

"It's time for you to go," I say, walking over to disarm the alarm.

"I'm not going anywhere. I gave you a chance and you didn't take it."

"A chance? You think killing my baby is a chance? What is wrong with you?"

"You!" she screams. "You're what's wrong with me. It's simple bitches like you who find pleasure in destroying somebody's else marriage. Well, you've picked the wrong one this time. Little girl, I've spent the last twenty-five years of my life making my husband into somebody, and if you think I'm going to hand him over to you, you're crazier than I am."

"Look lady, I don't want your husband. And for the record, he came to me. Hell, did you remind him that he was married because obviously he forgot. Wasn't he the one you took vows with? If you should be mad at anybody, it's him."

"No bitch! You're to blame. Had you kept your legs closed, we wouldn't have this problem. Did you honestly think I would let you bring my husband's baby into the world, making me a laughing stock of this city?"

"He doesn't even know I'm pregnant so stop with all the threats. I have no intention on telling him nor do I want him. So why don't you leave and we'll never talk about it again?"

"It's too late for that. I gave you a choice, but now it's time for you to pay. I will not allow you to have what I worked so hard for."

"Have you not heard anything I said? I. DON'T. WANT. YOUR. HUSBAND!" I scream.

"I know, because you won't get him. I'll be damned if you and this bastard child will reap the benefits of my harvest. No honey, you won't get the chance."

"How did you know I was pregnant anyway? No one knows but my doctor and Merci."

"That doesn't matter anymore."

"You're crazy and it's time for you to leave," I say, turning to open the door while dialing Merci's number. When she doesn't answer, I start to dial 911.

Before I can speak, I feel a sharp pain in the back of my head. Falling to the floor, she continues to hit me. I try to curl into a ball to protect my stomach from her kicks but she continues to deliver blow after blow.

The last thing I remember is her whispering, *"Tell my husband hello when you meet him in hell."*

Merci

After showering I try Grayce again and she still isn't answering. I'm getting worried because I had a missed call from her. She could be asleep but she should hear the phone. I try to shake the feeling of something bad happening to her so I decide to Facetime Thomas.

"Hey boo, you asleep?"

"Girl, you know I've been waiting on your call. How are you?"

"I'm good but I'm worried about Grayce. She called me earlier and I was in a meeting. Then I had a missed call from her about an hour ago but now she isn't answering. I've tried to call her twice and she still hasn't answered."

"Babe, you've got to stop worrying so much, she's probably asleep. Do you want me to go by there tonight?"

"No, you're probably right. I just don't like her being there by herself with everything going on."

"I'm sure she's fine, babe, but I'll go if you want me to."

"No, that's ok. I know you're still at work. She'll call me back when she wakes up. I'm being overly protective. Anyway, how was your day?"

"It was good, business as usual. How did everything go with the case? Any closer to finding out who it is?"

"Actually, the investigation is finally over!" I exclaim. "It was the head of accounting, Landon, responsible for all this. And you'd never guess that she was sleeping with the detective I was working with."

"You're kidding? Wow! What did he say when he found out?"

"He was pissed off! Babe, you should have seen his face," I laugh.

"That's crazy."

"Yes it is, but the great part is, she's in jail and I've already booked my flight home and packed my bags. I cannot wait to get home to my bed."

"That's great, babe, you have put in a lot of work on this case. But I have one question for you?"

"Ok?"

"Is your bed all that you're missing?"

"Um, I'm pretty sure that's about it. Why do you ask?"

"Don't play with me," he says laughing.

"Boy, you know I miss you. I cannot wait to taste those lips."

"I miss you too and I cannot wait for you to taste them. Now, what do you have on under that robe?"

"This old thing? Um, let's see," I say, smiling while untying the robe and letting it fall on one side to expose my breast.

"Hmm, keep going," he says, sitting up in the bed.

"Nah, I don't feel like it. I'll call you in the morning," I laugh.

"Girl, if you don't stop playing."

"You're at work."

"And I'm in my office, now continue."

Propping the iPad between my legs, I remove the robe showing there was nothing underneath but bare skin.

"Is this what you want, sir?"

"No, I want you but until then I settle for this. Now, open your legs wider."

"Like this?"

"Yea."

"What else do you want?"

"I want you to rub it."

"Rub what? Say it."

"Rub your clit," he says as I move my hand closer to it.

"Like this?" I ask, moving my fingers back and forth.

"Yea," he says, as I hear him unzip his pants. "Yes, just like that. Dang girl, see what you're doing to me," he asks as he moves his phone so that I can now see his rock hard penis.

"Hmm, I want you to put it inside of me," I moan as I watch him stroke it. Leaning back, I spread the lips of my vagina inserting a finger inside. "Put it inside of me."

I hear him moan as I continue to slide my fingers in and out.

"You want this dick?"

"Yes!"

"How do you want it?"

"Give it to me, hard! Um, just like that!" I tell him, rubbing myself harder.

"Shit Merci! Cum for me."

"Mmmm."

"Yes, make it cum for me. It's so juicy."

"Oh! I'm cumming!"

I hear him moan and grunt as the phone drops.

Leaning back on the bed, I gasp, "Babe! Thomas, are you alright?"

"Hell no! After that, I can't even think. Merci Alexander, I cannot wait to make you my wife so that I can make love to you for real."

"Well, you'll just have to make that happen, sir."

"That I will."

"Goodnight baby. I'll call you when I get up in the morning."

"Sweet dreams."

Disconnecting the call, I wash up before calling it a night.

4:56 AM – May 13

"Yea," I answer the phone, rolling back over into the bed. "Hello."

"Merci!" my mom screams.

"Yes Mother, what's wrong now?" I reply in my groggy voice.

"It's Grayce," she wails.

"What's Grayce?"

"She, she…" Mom stutters.

"Mom, it's early. Can I call you back when I get up?"

"She, uh, Grayce was attacked."

Springing up in the bed, I scream, "Attacked? Is she okay?"

"I don't know," she cries.

"What do you mean? Where is she?"

"We're at Regional One. The doctors don't know much yet. All they've said is that it doesn't look good. Merci, you need to get here, please!"

"I'm on my way."

I get up and quickly dress, grabbing my bags that I packed last night. I call the airport to see about changing to an earlier flight from New York back home to Memphis. Thank God I am able to get on the 6:30am one. I say a quick prayer for my sister as I rush to check out of the hotel.

After an almost three-hour flight, I finally make it to my car in long-term parking at the airport. Throwing my bags in, I jump into the driver's seat. Doing over 90 mph on the expressway I reach the hospital. I find a parking spot, quickly turn off the car engine and run inside.

"May I help you?" the receptionist asks as I walk into complete chaos.

"Yes ma'am, I'm looking for a patient's room, Grayce Alexander."

"Alexander," she says, tapping on the keyboard with a pace slower than a snail.

"Yes, G-R-A-Y-C-E Alexander."

"Here she is. She's in the trauma bay. Go down to the double doors and I'll buzz you in. Then you will need to go to the nurses' station on your left and they will be able to help further."

Going through the doors, I power walk to the nurses' station. Before I make it, I hear Mom call my name.

Running to her, I ask, "Mom, how is she?"

"It's really bad. They are prepping her for surgery."

"Surgery? No, they can't. Where's the doctor?"

"You just missed him by twenty minutes."

"I'll be back," I say, leaving her standing there.

Getting to the nurses' station, I let the nurse on duty know who I am and I ask her to page the doctor who is handling Grayce's chart. After what seems like forever, he calls back. The nurse hands me the phone.

"This is Dr. Felix."

"Dr. Felix, my name is Merci Alexander. I was told you're the one taking care of my sister Grayce. Can you please tell me what's going on? My mom says you're taking her to surgery but she's pregnant?"

"Yes ma'am, we became aware of her pregnancy when we performed an ultrasound of her abdomen, but right now she's very critical. Your sister suffered some cracked ribs and blunt force trauma to her face and head. The trauma has caused some bleeding on her brain and surgery is the only option we have to save her life."

"Oh my God. What about the babies?"

"As of now, they are stable and haven't been affected by Ms. Alexander's trauma. There's no sign of oxygen deprivation but I won't lie to you. This isn't going to be easy. I will do my best to save your sister but I have to ask, if it comes down to choosing between your sister and the babies—"

"Save my sister."

"Very well. It is my hope to save them all but I won't make you a promise I can't keep. Now, I have to go. The nurses will keep you updated throughout the surgery and I will be out to speak to you as soon as we're done."

"Thank you, doctor."

Walking back to where my parents are, I remember to call Thomas. With everything going on, I hadn't even thought about it until now.

He answers, still half asleep. "Babe, is everything alright? I thought your flight wasn't until later."

"Thomas, Grayce is hurt. She's at Regional One being prepped for surgery."

"I can be there in a few minutes. What time is your flight?"

"I'm already home, I took an earlier flight when my mom called. I've been here about fifteen minutes," I say trying to hold back my tears.

"Ok, I'm on the way."

Hanging up, I see Mom is standing there.

"Merci, what did the doctor say?"

"They're taking her to surgery. He said the nurses will keep us updated."

"That's it? Is she awake? Is she talking? What?"

"Mom, calm down. He didn't say any of that. All he said is that she needs surgery as soon as possible."

"I knew we shouldn't have left her."

"Left her where?"

"At your house."

"Are you kidding me, right now? Of all things to say, you picked this? I didn't make Grayce stay with me, she chose to. Furthermore, what does my house have to do with any of this?"

"That's where she was attacked."

"What? By who?"

"I don't know."

"Well, what are the police saying?"

"Nothing yet."

"You're not making sense, Mother, what happened?" I ask, getting agitated.

"I don't have all the details. Apparently Grayce dialed 911 while she was being attacked. They were able to trace the call to your address but by the time they got there, whoever did this was gone. They left my baby sprawled on the living room floor covered in blood. They left her there to die."

"This is crazy. How would someone get in without the alarm going off?"

"I don't know."

"Well, how did you all find out?"

"One of the officers at the scene is a member of the church. He called us once he recognized her. Merci, I just don't understand why this would happen to her. Grayce would never hurt anyone. Who would do something like this to her?"

"I did," a voice says from behind us.

Turning around, my Mom's eyes open wide in shock.

"You? Why would you hurt my baby?" Mom screams.

The woman standing there calmly states, "Because she was fucking my husband!"

Mom looks like she's about to pass out.

"I'm sorry, who are you?" I ask.

"My name is Shaunta Blair, and you must be the whore's sister?"

"Excuse you? What did you say?"

"You heard me. Don't act surprised, you know your sister is a whore. Sleeping around with other people's husbands. She had to know there would be consequences to her actions."

"Lady, you're talking crazy. Who in the hell is your husband?"

"Pastor Darrick Blair. D-A-R-R-I-C-K B—" she starts screaming.

"Girl, lower your damn voice. I didn't ask you to spell his name but please help me understand why you felt the need to hurt my sister over the actions of a grown man."

"She was the one sleeping with MY husband. She did this and she got what she deserved!"

"No! No! You're wrong, she was engaged to your son, for God's sake," my mom shouts. "This doesn't make sense. Why did you hurt my baby?"

"Come on Mrs. Alexander, open your eyes. Your daughter and my husband have been lying for months, carrying on an affair right under our noses. Who do you think she's pregnant by?"

"Now I know you're wrong. Grayce isn't the one pregnant, Merci is. Tell her!" my dad shouts at me. "Tell her you're the one who's the whore!"

She laughs. "You can't be that stupid. Damn! This whole family is a bunch of idiots."

"You're a liar!" Dad screams. "My Grayce wouldn't have done this."

She laughs, louder this time. "Your hoe of a daughter didn't give a damn about hurting me so I didn't give a damn about hurting her. She got what she deserved."

Before I can stop myself, I have both hands around her neck. "You got the audacity to show up here after beating my sister's head in and you think she deserved that? Bitch, I ought to choke the life out of you."

"Go ahead," she struggles to say. "I have nothing else to live for."

"Merci, stop! Merci, please don't kill her!" my mom yells as security comes running up. "Please Merci, let her go."

I release her and she slides to the floor coughing and trying to breathe as some nurses run towards her. Security grabs me.

"Let me go," I say, snatching away from them.

Thomas comes running in, "Merci, what is going on? Are you ok?"

"She was the one who attacked Grayce."

"What? Who is she?"

"Pastor Blair's wife."

"So is he the daddy—"

"Who in the hell knows? I come from a family that lies so they wouldn't know the truth if Jesus Himself showed up with it."

"I'm so sorry, babe." He hugs me and I don't know whether to cry or scream.

"How is Grayce?"

"She's in surgery. The doctor said she suffered blunt force trauma to the head and has bleeding on the brain. I knew something was wrong when she didn't answer my calls last night."

"This is not your fault."

"I know but—"

"No but, you couldn't have known this would happen."

The phone in the waiting room rings.

"Alexander family?" a lady yells out.

I run to the phone.

"This is her sister."

"This is Nurse Walton. The surgery has started and everything is going great so far. If all goes according to plan, the doctor should be done in about four hours. I will update you in another hour."

"Thank you."

I let Mom know what the nurse said before taking my seat next to Thomas. Laying my head on his shoulder, he nudges me to take a look at the TV screen.

BREAKING NEWS

"The body of a man found in a burning car on last night has been identified as forty-six year old Darrick Blair. Blair, an associate pastor of Emmanuel Grace Church, was found by Memphis Police after an anonymous report of a suspicious fire. There has been no official cause of death released but we will continue to keep you updated. Our thoughts and prayers are with his family."

Six hours later

Grayce is still in surgery so we are camped out in the family waiting area. At the last update, the doctor was almost done, but that was an hour ago. The police finally showed up to arrest Shaunta Blair but the doctors recommended placing her on suicide watch.

The detectives had fifty questions, none of which I could answer. I asked them about my sister's case and they stated someone would be back to speak to me.

"What's taking so long?" I ask out loud to no one in particular.

Just then the nurse comes through the doors still in the scrubs from surgery.

"Alexander family?"

I jump up along with my mom, my dad and Thomas. "How is she?"

"Would you all follow me down to the family room?"

We walk in to see two doctors sitting at the end of the table. One of which is Grayce's OBGYN and I presume Dr. Felix.

"My name is Dr. Marco Felix and I am head of neurosurgery here at Regional One. Are you the sister I spoke too?"

"Yes, my name is Merci Alexander."

"Ms. Alexander, This is my colleague Dr. Mara Baker, an OBGYN doctor who was already caring for Ms. Alexander."

"Yes, we've met."

"Please have a seat. As I told you earlier, your sister needed surgery to stop the bleeding from the blunt force trauma she received. And although we did all we could—"

"Oh God, no!" Mom wails.

"Please doctor," my dad says, "please don't tell me my daughter didn't survive."

Clearing his throat, he continues. "Mr. Alexander, your daughter suffered a traumatic brain injury and although we did everything we could to stop the bleeding, her brain began to swell. We were able to get it under control but she suffered a stroke."

"Ok, what does that mean? Will she have some paralysis or long term effects, what?" I ask.

"Ma'am, your sister isn't going to survive. Right now, she's been kept alive by machines. She is in what we call a maternal somatic coma."

"I don't understand? Is she alive or dead?"

"It means, her body is only being kept alive for the sake of the babies."

"Babies?" my daddy repeats.

"Yes sir, Ms. Alexander is about nineteen weeks pregnant and all we can do at this point is continue the life-saving measures in the hopes her babies survive. If we do, you have to understand that this will be of no benefit to your daughter. She is no longer breathing on her own and there is no active brain function. You all will need to decide if you like for us to continue these measures."

"Yes," I answer. "If there is nothing more you can do for my sister then yes please, save her babies."

"Hold on!" Dad screams. "How in the hell can you make a decision like that? You have no right! There has to be something else that can be done to save Grayce and if that means losing those babies, so be it!"

"I understand your frustration, sir, but there is nothing else we can do for your daughter. We've conducted testing such as an apnea test, checked for pupil reflexes and pain stimulation and they all tell us that Ms. Alexander has experienced brain death. I am so sorry."

"I won't believe that. I serve a God who is capable of reviving the dead. I don't care what your report says, I am believing the report of my God!" Dad shouts.

I cut my dad off. "Dr. Felix, how long can she be in this coma without compromising the babies?" I ask.

"I will let Dr. Baker answer that."

"We don't know for sure. Being pregnant while in a coma isn't common but it can happen. However, we won't know how her body will perform or even if the babies will survive. The only way to be sure is to take it week by week, monitoring for any signs of infection or possible miscarriage. As long as her body remains stable, she can be kept alive until the babies reach a viable gestational age."

"And when is that?"

"Thirty-two weeks is our hope because it gives them a greater chance of survival."

"What are the downsides?"

"There's the possibility of birth defects or fetal death. However, if you choose to proceed with this method, the longer the babies remain in utero, the less chance they'll have of any complications. But again, we won't know for sure until they are delivered. If her body makes it to thirty-two weeks, the chances of them surviving increases to between eighty and ninety-eight percent."

"Wow, this is a lot of information."

"Yes it is and if you need time to think, we can give you that."

"No, I don't need any time. If there's a chance you can save the babies, then yes, do it."

"Yes ma'am. We will do everything we can."

"Can I see my sister now?"

"Of course. I will leave you my card. If you think of anything, please call," Dr. Baker says.

Dr. Felix stands. "I will take you to your sister but you must prepare yourself for what you will see. She is very swollen and bruised and will not look like the person you are used to seeing. She will have a tube in her throat and there are also a lot of monitors connected to her. Although she has no brain function, she will still be warm to the touch and it may look as if she is breathing on her own but the machine is doing all the work."

Merci

Making it to the door of ICU Room 11, I stop. Mom and Dad are ahead of me so I allow them to go in first. After a few seconds, I hear a blood curdling scream from my mom. I lean against the door to stop myself from sliding onto the floor.

Thomas grabs me as my dad is bringing my mom out in his arms. The nurses quickly run to her because she's passed out.

"Babe?"

"Give me a minute."

I push myself up and turn the small corner into her room. Seeing all the machines, I feel my knees buckling.

"We don't have to go right at this moment," Thomas whispers to me.

"I have to," I say as I walk towards the bed.

Looking upon her unrecognizable face, I begin sobbing as I rub her. "Why did she do this to you? What am I going to do without you?"

Thomas pushes a chair up behind me as I sit beside her bed. Holding her hand, I start to hum Jennifer Hudson's song, *'Jesus Promised Me a Home'*. I don't know why it came to me but I can't stop and neither will the tears.

Thomas, rubbing my shoulders, begins to pray.

"God, we may not understand but have your way. Whatever your will is, let it be done. But please oh God, give strength to this family now. Even when they can't seem to comprehend, send a peace that quiets their screams and calms their fears. Lord God, have your way and we dare not complain because when we think back, we know that Grayce is your creation and you don't owe us an explanation for coming to take what belongs to you. Dispatch your angels to encamp around her bedside. Cover and protect these babies until their time of birth shall arrive. And guide the doctors and nurses. God, I pray. Amen."

As I listen to him, I lay my head on the bed and weep.

=====

Feeling something on my head, I open my eyes to see Grayce's eyes open.

"Grayce," I shout, while jumping up from the chair. "You came back."

Blinking her eyes, I wipe the tears that are sliding from them.

"Don't try to talk because you have this tube in. I'll get the doctor." But she moves her hand to mine. She blinks and then motions for something to write with. I look around for Thomas but he's not there. I run over to the area by the sink and find a notepad and a pen.

Rushing back to her side, I place the pen in her hand while I hold the pad. She scribbles … 'bab.'

"The babies?" I say and she blinks. "They are fine. They are strong and fighting."

She blinks again and starts to write again. 'Papers home.'

"Papers home? What do you mean?"

She points at the words again.

"You left some papers at home?" She blinks. "For who?"

She slowly points at me.

"What kind of papers?"

She points at the first thing she wrote.

"For the babies?"

She blinks.

"I don't understand."

She begins to write again. 'Read.'

"I will but let me get the doctors to take this tube out."

She blinks and moves her head no.

"Yes. The doctors were wrong. You're going to be just fine."

She shakes her head no again and I realize ...

"You can't leave me."

She scribbles, 'Love u.'

I begin to cry. "You can't leave me. We just started rebuilding our relationship. Now you want me to let you go? I can't. Please sister, please don't leave me."

She beckons for me to read the paper again.

"I love you too," I say, almost at a whisper.

She blinks and then closes her eyes as the machines began to cry out.

"No Grayce! No, don't go, please!"

"Merci, Merci, baby wake up," Thomas says, shaking me.

I jump up and look at Grayce still lying there.

"Baby," Thomas says.

"I thought she woke up," I say, walking into his arms. "I thought she—"

"I know but it was just a dream."

I scream out, "Why my sister? Please God!" I didn't even realize I was screaming so loud and hitting Thomas until he grabs my arms and nurses come running in. I fall onto the floor.

"Dr. Harvey, would you like us to give her something to calm her down?"

"Not yet, give me a minute," he says.

"This hurts so much," I cry. "Why did it have to be her?"

He doesn't say anything as he rubs my back.

"What am I supposed to do? What am I supposed to do without her?"

"All you can do is take one day at a time."

I cry in his arms.

=====

I open my eyes and look around not even remembering where I am.

When I try to sit up, my head is hurting so bad.

"Babe, hold on. Let me help you," Thomas says.

"Where am I?"

"You're in one of the on-call rooms at the hospital."

When he says this, the events of the evening come rushing back.

"I thought this was a bad dream. Is she really gone?"

"Yes, she's gone," he replies before climbing in the bed behind me.

"How long was I asleep?"

"A few hours. I had the nurses give you something to sleep because you were so hysterical."

"What time is it?"

"Almost 3am. Dr. Baker stopped by to drop off some paperwork for you. She'll be back tomorrow morning around ten to discuss the options for Grayce."

Then I remembered the dream, causing me to jump up. Wincing in pain from the headache I have, I tell Thomas that I need to go home.

"Can it wait, you really need to rest."

"No, I have to go now."

=====

Pulling up to the house, the yellow crime scene tape is still across the front door.

"Are you sure you want to do this?"

"Yes, I have to. Grayce left something for me."

"How do you know that?"

"I just know."

Getting out the car, I walk to the garage and put the code in to let the door up. I enter the house and go through the laundry room, which has an entrance to a closet off of my master bathroom.

"Babe, where are you going?" Thomas asks, following close behind me.

"To my room."

I walk as fast as I can through my bathroom and then into my bedroom. I stop when I see a folder on my bed. I run over and grab it, spilling the contents out. There are insurance papers, a will, some bank papers and a handwritten letter.

I sit on the bed contemplating whether to read it now or later.

"Babe, do you want me to leave you alone?"

"No, please stay."

I sigh. Before I can even get it open good I start crying.

"You don't have to read it tonight. You've already been through enough."

"I need too."

May 12, 2016

Dear Merci,

When I showed up at your house, a year ago, you should have slammed the door in my face and I wouldn't have blamed you. Even after everything you went through because of me, you should have hated me yet you still opened your home to me. It didn't make sense to me then but I now know it was God working in you. Thank you. Thank you for being obedient to Him and not giving up. No matter how hard it was living with me, you didn't give up on me.

Sister, I need you to know that I am sorry. Sorry for everything. Growing up with you was the best thing to happen to me and I'm so blessed to have been able to call you sister. I know we've missed a lot of years but I'm grateful that God allowed us time to mend the broken pieces of our relationship, if only for a little while. Thank you for loving me even when it hurt.

Now, if you're reading this letter, it means I'm no longer with you. Don't be upset, it was my time. I don't know how, why, when or where but that doesn't matter anymore. God spoke to me yesterday and He promised everything would be okay. He said you'd be alright without me because He's leaving a piece of me with you, my baby girl. As for my baby boy, he couldn't live without me.

I love you Merci Renee Alexander and I know you'll make a wonderful wife and mother. And although I will not be there physically, I'll always be with you in spirit. I won't tell you not to grieve but don't grieve too long because you have a life to live and you can't do that crying. Sister, I don't know what tomorrow holds but promise me, you'll never take another day for granted.

You are sole beneficiary as well as having the power of attorney to handle all medical decisions. I've also left you specific instructions for my funeral, FOLLOW THEM! I don't care what Mom or Dad says.

Oh, Thomas is your husband so don't you dare run that fine man off. Let him love your broken pieces and pull you through this pain. You're going to need him. Plus, you're going to need a baby daddy. LOL!

I love you, always and forever Merci.

Your baby sister Grayce

P.S. I'm sorry for leaving you to deal with our parents but I have no doubt you can handle it. XOXO

I pull the letter up to my chest, crying and laughing at the same time. Thomas pulls me into his arms.

"When I left my parents' home, I thought it was the worst pain I could feel but this, it hurts down to my core. It's a pain I wouldn't wish on anybody. I mean, one minute I'm watching a sonogram of new life inside her belly and now she's gone. Life can be so funny, you know, and it has a way of changing even without permission," I say before sitting up and wiping my face. "Do you mind taking me to a hotel?"

"A hotel?" he asks, confused.

"Yea, I cannot stay here."

"I know but I thought you'd come home with me."

I look at him.

"Merci, you can't honestly think I'm going to allow you to stay at a hotel by yourself. Besides, you need me. Let me love your broken pieces."

"What did you just say?"

"I said, let me love your broken pieces."

I look at him and smile. "God has a way of doing things, you know?"

"What do you mean?"

"Read this," I say, handing him Grayce's letter while I go to pack a bag.

After I finish packing some clothes and toiletries, I come out to find him sitting on the side of the bed. He looks up but doesn't say anything as tears now flow down his face.

I kneel in front of him. "That night you prayed for me, I couldn't explain the feeling it gave me nor how you could possibly know I'd be your wife. Yes, I know God and the fact He works in mysterious ways, but everything has been happening so fast. But when you said what you said a few minutes ago, I know without a doubt, this is all God. I've never had a man to truly love me, not even my dad, but then you show up at the very time all hell is breaking loose in my life, ready to love every part of me; good and bad, broken and whole."

This time I wipe the tears from his face.

"Merci Alexander, can I love your broken pieces and help pull you through this pain?" he asks.

All I can do is nod my head yes.

"Babe, do you know what she meant about the baby boy?" Thomas asks.

"No. I just assume it was a mistake."

"Ok. Well, let's get out of here. You need to try and sleep."

10:00 AM – Meeting with Dr. Baker

"Good morning Merci," Dr. Baker says meeting us, again, in the family room.

"Dr. Baker, thank you for meeting with us this morning. These are my parents, Gina and Melvin Alexander. You already know my boyfriend, Dr. Harvey, right?"

"Yes. Dr. Harvey, it's good seeing you again, and Merci you don't have to thank me, I am here to ensure your sister and her babies receive the best care possible. As Dr. Felix advised on last night, your sister is in what's called a maternal somatic coma which means she is being kept alive for the sake of the unborn babies. It is our hope her body sustains the pregnancy until at least thirty-two weeks."

"Is there a chance her body will reject the pregnancy?" I ask.

"Not necessarily but there are risks associated with keeping her in a coma. She can get a condition called hemodynamic instability which can cause an abnormal blood pressure that can affect her organs. She can get an infection or multiple other things that will be hard for us to medicate due to the pregnancy. However, only time will tell if any of these will present."

"What if we choose not to keep her on life support?" my dad asks.

"We will have to abide by your wishes."

"Hold on, we are not taking her off life support," I say.

"Says who?" Dad counters. "Who are you to decide what happens with Grayce's life? You've been back in her life all of six months and now you get to decide if she remains hooked up to machines? No! You have no right to make these decisions. As a matter of fact, you can leave. I didn't want you here anyway. I don't know why Gina even called you."

"Melvin!" my mother screams. "This is not the time."

"When is the time, Gina? When this girl leaves our daughter on her death bed for months? No! I won't stand for it. She will not have that say. Hell, she can't even take care of her own life."

I'd had enough. I was sitting there shaking with my fists balled up, ready to knock him on his ass. I put my hands on the arm of the chair to get up when Thomas stops me.

"Mara, does your paperwork show who has the power of attorney for Ms. Alexander's medical decisions?"

"Um, yes I believe so. Give me a second."

"And who the hell are you?" Dad says, turning to Thomas.

"My name is Dr. Thomas Harvey."

"Oh, you're still around? I thought with the way Merci goes through men you'd be gone by now."

"That's enough, Dad."

"I'm just getting started, little girl."

"No, you're just leaving. Dr. Baker, you don't have to look at your paperwork because I have my own and it clearly states that Grayce wanted me in charge of all her affairs. So, if you'd excuse me while I show this asshole out." I stand and go over to the door and open it. "Mom, you are more than welcome to stay but your husband isn't."

"I'm not going anywhere. This is my damn daughter!" he yells.

"Thomas, can you call security."

My dad jumps up and so does Thomas, who walks over to where I am. Dad starts laughing.

"You've always been an ungrateful, lowdown bitch. And you," he says turning to Thomas, "who are you, captain save a hoe? Haven't you heard you can't turn a hoe into a housewife?"

"You need to leave, sir," Thomas says.

"Oh, I'm leaving but I'll be back with my lawyer. Come on, Gina."

"I'm not going," she says, clutching her purse tighter.

"What did you say to me?"

"You heard me. I'm not leaving."

"You need to get up now!" His voice booms off the walls. "You've been around this girl for all of an hour and now you want to speak to me that way. Get your stuff and let's go!"

"I told you, I'm not leaving."

He just stands there and laughs.

"This way, sir," Thomas says, directing him to the door.

"I'll be back. Just watch!"

I shake my head while heading back to my seat. "Dr. Baker, I am sorry you had to be witness to that."

"You don't have to apologize. When it comes to families and the emotions of dealing with someone who's sick, I've seen far worse. Trust me, I get it."

"What do we do next?" Mom asks.

"We wait. I know it doesn't sound like much but that's all we can do at this point. We have another thirteen weeks to go. I won't lie, it's going to be a long, hard journey and it's going to be very expensive as her insurance will not cover everything."

"I don't care about the cost," I tell her. "Do what you have to do to grant my sister's wish of saving her babies."

"Absolutely. I'll be around later today to check on things."

After Dr. Baker leaves, I place my head in my hands and sigh. My mom reaches over and puts her hand on my arm. I flinch at her touch.

"What could I have possibly done to make him treat me like this?"

"Huh?"

"Why does my own father treat me like I'm an alien from another planet? Am I not the same daughter he used to call the apple of his eye? The same one he told he'd love until his dying day? Well, what changed? What happened, Mother? The least you can do is tell me."

"I don't know."

"You're a liar. This entire family is a bunch of liars, even Grayce, and look how it worked out for her. And you still sit here covering for him. Well, that's okay, I won't push today but believe me I will because it's the only way you will be involved in your grandchildren's lives."

Three weeks later – June 3

Grayce has been moved to a long term ICU unit. Her room is filled with flowers and balloons from people sending their respects. I've been playing gospel music from our local gospel station, 95.7 Hallelujah FM, even though I know Grayce probably can't hear it but I think it's more for me anyway.

I've been praying a lot lately, asking God for strength to deal with all of this because it's been quite a journey. Watching my sister lie here knowing I'll have to say goodbye to her in a few weeks isn't the only thing. Oh no, I've also had to deal with my asshole of a dad who has been trying everything possible to have Grayce removed from the breathing machine. Every other day I am being served with some type of paperwork from his lawyer. Nothing has worked but it doesn't stop him from trying.

Some days it feels like it's too much but then I read 2 Corinthians 12:9 that says, *'But he said to me, "My grace is sufficient for you, for my power is made perfect in weakness." Therefore I will boast all the more gladly of my weaknesses, so that the power of Christ may rest upon me.'* And I realize that at my weakest, I am yet strong because God is with me. It also helps that I have Thomas. He's been one of the greatest joys these past weeks. I don't know what I would have done without him.

"Good morning," a voice from the door says.

"Hey."

"My name is Detective Craig Harris from the Memphis Police Homicide Department."

I get up and walk to him, extending my hand. "It's nice to meet you."

"I'm sorry to bother you but I wanted to ask you some questions regarding your sister's case. Do you have time to speak to me?"

"Sure. Do you mind if we take a walk, I need some fresh air?"

"Of course."

We find a coffee cart outside and purchase a drink before finding a bench to sit on.

Detective Harris has a lot of questions, most of which I can't answer. He asked if I knew how long Grayce's affair was with Darrick. I don't. Hell, I don't know anything, and it's not because I didn't want to but it was because Grayce was good at lying.

He understands, I don't.

"Detective, why has it taken so long regarding Grayce's case?"

"With everything going on and your sister being unable to talk, we've had to do a lot of investigative work. I'm sorry it has taken me this long to reach out to you. I have spoken to your parents a few times."

"We've not been on the best of speaking terms."

"I understand," he says.

"Do you know how Shaunta Blair was able to get into the house without the alarm going off? Did Grayce let her in?"

"From our investigation, it looks like she was already there when your sister got home. We found her fingerprints throughout the house, and also some items she dropped in a closet in the hallway."

"Wait, this doesn't make sense. Why didn't she set the alarm off?" Pulling my phone from my pocket, I scroll through the security company's app and stop.

"What is it?" he asks.

"She forgot to set the alarm before she left for work. Dammit, Grayce."

He jots the info down in his notepad.

"How would she have known this though?" I ask.

"This lady was watching your sister's every move. All it took was one slip up from your sister for her to get close, and unfortunately, she found it. Ms. Alexander, you have to understand, when it comes to domestic cases like this women who are out for revenge will do anything necessary to get it. Your sister was her target and once she got her locked in, she was determined by any means necessary to make her pay."

"Is this how she knew Grayce was pregnant? She was the one stalking her, right?"

"Yes. I shouldn't be telling you this but during the course of our investigation, we found out that Mrs. Blair's sister worked in the doctor's office."

"Wow."

"I know this is hard for your family but I can assure you, we are working hard to make sure Mrs. Blair is fully prosecuted for this as well as anyone else involved."

"Thank you. I just wish Grayce would be able to see it."

"What do you mean? If you don't mind me asking," he asks.

"She's brain dead, only being kept alive for the sake of the babies."

"I am so sorry, I didn't know. The doctor wouldn't give me any information and your dad didn't relay that when I talked to him last."

"I understand. Just make sure she pays."

"We will. Here's my card. If there's anything you can think of or if you have any questions, please don't hesitate to call."

"Oh, detective, do you know when my house will be released?"

"Not yet. More than likely in a few weeks."

"Thanks."

"I'll be in touch."

Merci

I head back to Grayce's room just as my dad is going in. I stand outside the door. I don't want to see him because it'll only lead to an argument.

I listen in as he talks to her. "My beautiful Grayce, I don't know why God allows things such as this to happen but I can't question Him. No matter how bad I want to, I can't, but I miss you, sweet girl."

He starts to cry which stuns me because he's yet to show any emotions.

"Why didn't you tell me you were pregnant? We could have dealt with this. Why?" he says, getting louder. "I'm so angry at you. You should have told me the mess you were in. I could have fixed it. You should—"

When I don't hear him speaking anymore, I look in and see his head laid on her chest as he sobs.

I move away from the door, shocked. My dad actually has feelings. I shake my head as I walk away until he leaves.

=====

"Good afternoon, Merci," Dr. Baker says walking into the room with a few nurses, one rolling an ultrasound machine.

"Anything wrong?" I ask, hurrying over to the side of the bed from the window seat I'd made my home away from home.

"No, I just want to make sure the babies are still doing fine."

Dr. Baker gives directions to the nurses as she slides Grayce's gown up. She is now twenty-two weeks and her stomach is getting bigger. It amazing to watch her still be able to give life even though she will never get a chance to experience feeling the babies move, giving birth or even raising them.

I move closer to the bed as she begins the ultrasound.

"It looks like we have an active little girl here," she says pointing to the screen. "She is measuring right on target for where she should be, almost a pound."

"What about the baby boy?"

"He's, hmm, give me a minute."

She continues the ultrasound for another few minutes, moving in all different directions. She finally finishes, wipes Grayce's belly and pulls her gown back down.

"Doctor?"

"Merci, I am going to be honest with you. I cannot find a heartbeat for Baby B. It looks like he didn't make it."

I move away from the bed and sit down. She pulls a chair in front of me.

"Merci, I am so sorry. It was my hope that both babies would survive. The blessing is that you still have a baby girl who is growing and very active. All we can do at this point is pray that she survives another eleven weeks. I wish there was more I could do."

"I understand Dr. Baker and I am appreciative of everything you're doing. What happens now to Baby B?"

"He will remain in the womb until it's time to deliver."

"Will that hurt the other baby?"

"At this point, there should be no complication to Baby A, but we will monitor her more closely to be sure. Again, I am sorry. The last thing I wanted to do was deliver more bad news."

"Thank you Dr. Baker," I say as my mom walks in.

"Doctor, is everything okay?" she asks, causing Dr. Baker to look at me.

"It's fine. I will explain everything to her. Thank you again."

"You're welcome. Here are pictures of Baby A. I'll leave you two alone."

"What happened?

"One of the babies died."

"Oh God, no! What about the other one?"

"She's still alive and healthy. Dr. Baker is hoping she'll hold out a little while longer."

"My poor baby," Mom says walking over to rub Grayce's face. "Why did it have to be you?"

"Were you hoping it was me?"

"Merci, I didn't mean it like that."

"Then what did you mean?

"Nothing, I don't want to argue."

"You know, I used to try to figure out what I could have possibly done to make you all hate me so much, but now I don't care. I have so much other stuff going on in my life that I can no longer carry the burden of you and Daddy. But you have to know that God has a way of bringing everything to the light. I just pray you'll be able to handle it when He does?"

"Not right now Merci, please."

"When then? Since I was fourteen, Dad has treated me like I have a contagious disease and you've allowed it. So cut the bullshit, Mother, and tell me what's going on."

"Merci?"

I turn to see Pastor Parker standing there. "Pastor Parker, I am so sorry you had to hear that."

"I'll be back to check on Grayce," my mother says, bolting for the door.

"Is everything alright?"

"No!" I say, breaking down in tears.

Pastor Parker takes me by the arm and guides me over to the chair. I sit and then he sits.

"I don't understand, Pastor Parker. Why do my own parents hate me? I've done nothing to them."

"Merci, sometimes the storms we fight and the things we have to deal with aren't even about us. I don't know your parents nor do I know the circumstance of their hatred but I can tell you this: everything that is done in the dark will eventually come to light. Psalm 119 says joy comes to those who keep their integrity, follow God's law and search for Him because when you do this, you won't compromise with evil. I know you're having it hard right now but it's not the time for you to crumble nor is it the time to hash out family drama. Your sister is counting on you to be strong. Keep your integrity and your joy will show up."

"I know but this is so hard."

"Yes, but you have to go through pain before you heal. You'll get through this but you've got to trust God to handle what you can't understand."

"I'm trying, I really am."

"It'll eventually get easier but until that time comes, you've got to go through it."

"Thank you, Pastor Parker."

"You don't have to thank me. I am here for you."

I reach over and hug him.

"Um, excuse me, I didn't mean to interrupt. I'll come back," Thomas says.

Pastor Parker releases me as I wipe the tears from my eyes.

"No babe, you don't have to go," I say getting up to hug him. He kisses me on the lips. "Thomas, you remember my pastor, Pastor Nathan Parker, right?"

"Yes, it's good to see you again, I just hate it's under these circumstances and not worshipping together," Pastor Parker says extending his hand.

"I agree," Thomas says, shaking his hand. "Is everything alright? I passed Dr. Baker in the hall."

"Yea, she did another ultrasound and couldn't find a heartbeat for Baby B."

"I'm so sorry, I should have been here with you."

"There was nothing you could have done. Besides, I can deal with that but what I cannot deal with is my parents. They make everything harder. Pastor Parker came in at the right time to offer some encouraging words."

"I'm glad I could be here for you all. Can we have a word of prayer before I leave?"

"Of course."

We stand around Grayce's bed. I hold her hand on one side as Pastor Parker places his hand on her stomach. He begins to pray.

"Our Father in Heaven, Lord, it is your humble servant petitioning your throne asking you to incline your ear to us at this hour. I know we aren't in a sanctuary but your word says where two or more are gathered together, touching and agreeing on the same thing, you'll be in the midst. Well God, we need you to come into this hospital room at Regional One and have your way. We don't know why things happen but we trust you. We don't have the answers but we know you are never wrong. So God, at this moment, may your will be done. Give strength to Merci so that she can stand even when it feels like she'll crumble. And cover this little

girl who is still growing, allowing her to get stronger until it is time for her to grace us with her presence. Keep this family now during this difficult time and keep the enemy at bay. Heal, oh God, what is broken and you deliver like only you can. We know you are a sustainer and we dare not question you but we put our trust in you knowing whatever your will is, shall be done. Lord, I pray. Amen."

We all say amen in unison.

"Thank you Pastor Parker. I really appreciate you coming by."

"No thanks needed. Sis. Parker and I will be by in a few days but if you need us before then, please don't hesitate to call me directly. Thomas, it was good seeing you."

When he leaves, Thomas sits in my chair by the window and pulls me down into his lap.

I lay my head on his shoulders and then all of a sudden, I jump up.

"Merci, what's wrong."

I run over to my bag.

"Babe, talk to me. What are you looking for?"

Pulling Grayce's letter from my bag, I begin reading it again. "As for my baby boy, he couldn't live without me," I read out loud. "She knew. Thomas, she knew he wouldn't survive. I didn't understand what this meant then but I do now."

I walk over to her bed and rub her stomach as Thomas walks up behind me. I don't say anything because I have no words. I simply allow his arms to comfort me.

Merci

August

For the two months, Baby Girl A has held on. Watching Grayce's stomach grow while it looks like she is asleep has been amazing and terrifying at the same time. Terrifying because I know that any day now, the doctors are going to wheel her in the operating room to deliver the babies, which means I'll finally have to let my sister go.

My mom and dad have still been visiting when I am not here and I'm fine with that.

I finally got the chance to meet Thomas' parents at our wedding. Oh, I forgot to mention that. Yes, on July 31, which happens to be Grayce's birthday, we decided to have a small ceremony in the chapel of the hospital. It was just me, him, his mom and dad and my pastor and wife. I decided to do it on Grayce's birthday because I knew she'd want me to celebrate on her day instead of mourning that she is no longer here.

Now, we're just waiting for Dr. Baker to decide on the day to deliver the babies. Although Baby B passed away, he still has to be delivered.

I am in my usual spot by the window when I hear someone clear their throat. I put down my Kindle and look up to see it's Warren.

"What are you doing here?"

"I am not here to cause any trouble."

"Then why are you here."

"Marie told me everything that's going on."

"So, what? You decided to stop by to see if it's true?"

"No. I don't know what made me show up here. I guess I just wanted to see her."

"Awl, that's sweet but the last time I remember seeing you, you had your hands around her throat so forgive me if I don't find your words genuine."

"I didn't come here to upset you. I wanted you to know that I am deeply sorry for what happened and that I've been praying for Grayce and for the baby."

"I don't need your empty prayers. However, what I do need is your parental rights terminated, if you are indeed the father to this baby."

"Can I think on it?"

"Yes, you can think up until the time the DNA test is back but please understand this: I will not allow you take my niece."

Just then the monitors in the room begin to beep.

The nurses come running in followed by Dr. Baker.

"Dr. Baker, what's wrong?"

"Grayce's blood pressure is dropping. We have to perform the surgery now to save the baby."

"But she's only thirty-one weeks."

"I know but we have to."

They are working as fast as they can to unhook the machines in order to get her to the operating room.

"I'll keep you updated," Dr. Baker says as she hurries out.

I look over at Warren who has this shocked look on his face.

"Merci, I'm—"

"Save it and please go."

=====

I'm pacing in the empty hospital room when Thomas comes in followed by my parents.

"Any word?" Mom asks.

"Not yet," I say as Thomas pulls me into his arms.

"God, please let the baby be okay," I say into the stillness of the air.

After what seems like forever, Dr. Baker finally comes in.

"She's great, Merci." She beams. "She weighs 3lbs, 7oz. but she's here."

"Oh thank you, Jesus. What about the other baby?"

"I delivered him as well. You can see him, if you want."

"Yes. I would like to see them both."

"Baby A is being taken to the NICU. She's early so she's considered a preemie. You will be able to see her in the nursery once they get her settled in. You can follow me down to see Baby B."

"What about Grayce?" Mom asks.

"She will be brought in shortly. Merci, I wanted to speak to you regarding organ donation because according to Grayce's records, she selected that option. Have you given any thoughts to it?"

"To be honest Dr. Baker, I haven't but if it's what she wanted—"

"No!" my dad shouts! "You will not do this. You will not cut out any of her organs. The bible says—"

"Save your speech for Sunday, Dad. Dr. Baker, if her organs are viable to save someone else's life, take them."

She nods her head and leaves the room.

"Why must you go against everything I say?" he demands through gritted teeth.

"You are of no concern to me. I'm granting Grayce's final request. If it happens to bother you, oh well."

"You are—"

I cut him off. "If I were you I'd shut up because you are already walking a thin line with me. I really don't care if I ever see you again but if you want to see your granddaughter, you'd better put your lips together and hush. Grayce may have taken your shit, but I am not her."

Thomas grabs my hand pulling me away from them as we head to see Grayce's baby boy.

Getting to the nursery, it feels like I am moving in slow motion. As I make it to the bassinet that is holding his small body, I blink back the tears. I reach in and pick him up. Looking into his sweet face, I wish things could have been different. "Rest on, sweet boy, and give your momma a kiss for me."

Rocking him, Thomas asks, "Do you have a name for him?"

"Not yet. Do you have a suggestion?"

"What about Ethan?"

"Ethan huh?"

I spend a little more time with him before handing him back to the nurse.

As we turn to leave, another nurse comes over placing a band on mine and Thomas' arm. This bands lists us as Baby A's guardians because this is what Grayce wanted. The nurse explains that the same kind of band will be placed on the baby and each time she is brought in or taken out, they will need to verify that our band matches hers.

I nod my understanding. She lets us know we should be able to visit her in about thirty minutes.

Thomas and I head back down to where my parents are. I ask them about seeing Ethan but they refuse. I shrug my shoulders: it's their loss. I try to sit but I am anxious to see the baby.

Grayce is finally brought in. The nurses work to hook up her machines. Dr. Baker comes back with papers for me to sign for the harvesting of Grayce's organs.

"Merci, it is up to you on when you will like the surgery to take place as you will need to say your final goodbyes before it. I will give you all some time to think about it."

I walk over to Grayce. "Sister, your babies are beautiful. I wish you could be here to see them. Thank you for leaving us a piece of you in your baby girl."

I bend over into the bed and kiss her face. Wiping my tears, I say, "Dr. Baker, give me two hours to make a few phone calls and then you can schedule the surgery. We've kept her from resting long enough. It's time we let her go."

"No," my mom cries. "I'm not ready."

Dr. Baker nods before leaving.

"Mom, you both can have your time. I'll come back in a little while," I say walking out.

Thomas catches up to me and grabs my hand.

"Babe, are you sure you want to do this now?"

"She's held on long enough. It has to be now or I may never do it."

"Is there anything you need me to do?"

"Can you let your parents know? I need them here."

"Of course."

He kisses me before leaving. I walk into the family waiting room and sit at the small table. I pull out my phone and Google the number for Harrison Funeral Home. I give them the details they need to pick up Grayce's and Ethan's bodies once they are released from the morgue. I call Pastor Parker, my boss and a few of Grayce's friends she worked with at Sycamore Elementary School, letting them all know she'll be removed from the machines in the next two hours, if they want to be here.

I say a prayer for strength before I leave out. I walk to the window of the nursery just as Dr. Baker is coming out.

"Oh Merci, I was coming to get you. You can see her now."

She gives me a gown to put on. I wash my hands and before I can even look at her properly, I start to cry. She has so many tubes. The nurse opens up the door of the incubator, I reach in and begin to rub her chest.

"Hey little lady, Happy Birthday. August 5, 2016 will be a day of celebration from now on. I'm your Auntie Merci and I'm so glad to finally meet you. You are a fighter just like your mom and I know she is proud of you. Now, I need you to continue to fight for me, you hear? You have to fight. Fight for your auntie because she needs you."

I remove my arm to allow the door to be closed.

"Merci, this is Dr. Mendez and she will be taking care of Baby Alexander."

"It's nice to meet you, Dr. Mendez.'

"Ms. Alexander, your niece was born at thirty-one weeks but she is a strong little girl. We will keep her here in the NICU for a few weeks as we work on getting her to eat, breathe and control body temperature without the help of machines. It is our hope that she is able to move from this incubator in a few days but only time will tell. You are more than welcome to visit her as it will benefit her greatly."

"Thank you Dr. Mendez. It is alright if my parents visit?"

"Sure."

I get back down to the room and let my parents know they can see Baby A now. Once they leave, Thomas says, "Babe, what are you going to name her? We can't keep calling her Baby A."

"Her name is Imani," I quickly answer.

"Imani, that means faith, right?"

"Yes. Because of that little girl, my faith is even stronger. Her name is Imani Grayce Alexander."

Saying goodnight

August 5, 2016

It's 7pm and we all gather to say our final goodbyes to Grayce and Ethan. I had him brought into the room and placed beside her. He is wrapped snugly in a blanket where we can only see his small face.

Dr. Felix and Dr. Baker arrive and I give them the signed paperwork that'll make everything final.

I walk over to Grayce's bed. "Sister, I know you are proud of your little girl. She is strong and a fighter like you. I wish you could see and hold her. I promised you I'd take care of her and I will. I will make sure she knows everything about you. Just the good, not the bad." I laugh. "I love you. Goodnight, sweet girl."

I give Mom and Dad another few minutes to say their goodbyes. I ask Pastor Parker to pray and in the midst Sis. Parker begins singing,

"When peace like a river, attendeth my way, When sorrows like sea billows roll. Whatever my lot, thou hast taught me to say, it is well, it is well, with my soul. It is well with my soul. It is well, it is well with my soul."

The machines are not turned off because she's an organ donor but it's final. I want to cry out for them but I know they are in a better place. I want to scream for them to stay but I know it's not possible. I even want to cry out to ask God 'why them' but it's not my place. They both belonged to God and He simply repossessed what was His. I can't be mad at Him for that.

Grayce's wake

Walking into the doors of Emmanuel Church makes me sick at the stomach. However, this is where Grayce wanted her visitation to be held. My dad pitched a fit to find out the funeral wouldn't be held here and nor would he be doing the eulogy, but I didn't care.

Gripping Thomas' hand tighter, I prepare myself to enter the sanctuary to view Grayce's body before anybody else.

"Whew!" I let out.

"You got this. Just put one foot before the other and breathe."

I stop and look around the sanctuary and I am blown away by how well the funeral home has taken care all of my requests. Yellow is… was Grayce's favorite color and they made sure a touch of yellow is in everything.

Walking up to the altar, to Grayce's casket, I can't do it. I stumble back into Thomas' arms as I let out a cry from the pit of my stomach.

"Oh God, why my sister? Why now, God? I miss her so much"

Some of the ushers are there as Thomas guides me to the nearest pew and lets me cry into his chest. One of the ushers stuffs some tissues into my hand while another one fans me. I've never understood the purpose of fanning someone who's crying but I don't even have the energy to tell her to stop.

By the time I sit up, it feels like I've been crying forever. My eyes hurt, my heart hurts, my soul hurts and there's no amount of medicine that can heal it.

I finally stand and walk back to the casket pausing at the small box that was specially made to fit beside Grayce that holds her baby boy who died at nineteen weeks.

After seeing him in the hospital we named him Ethan Renee Alexander which was engraved on his little white and yellow casket. I rub my hand across his name as I look upon the face of my beautiful baby sister. Standing there makes it so real and it snatches the air from my lungs.

I grab hold of the casket as I look at her. The bruises that were once there have long healed and the funeral home's makeup artist has done an amazing job. She is beautiful with her long black hair perfectly styled like she usually wore it. It's as if she is simply sleeping but the pain I feel reminds me that she isn't.

The tears fall symbolizing the many days and nights we've missed of each other's lives, the future she'll never see, her baby girl she'll never raise, the baby boy who died too soon and for all the anger I once held for her. I cry and I rub my hand over her chest. AND. I. CRY.

"I miss you so much."

I turn into Thomas but I don't want to be hugged anymore. I just need a moment to myself.

"I'll be back."

Walking out of the sanctuary, I run into Shaun.

"Merci, I am so sorry for your loss."

"Why are you sorry?" I ask wiping my tears.

"I, uh, I don't know. I thought it was the most appropriate thing to say."

"Well, it's not."

"Look, I know you're angry with my family and I don't blame you. I only came to pay my respects to Grayce, not upset you and your family."

"Shaun, I am not angry at you. Everything that happened and the reason my sister and her baby boy is lying in a casket right now instead of being here with us raising her daughter is because of your mother and father. You aren't to blame."

"Wait, Grayce had a baby?"

"Yea. Didn't your mom tell you? She'd been stalking Grayce for weeks prior to beating her head in. She was mad because she wouldn't have an abortion."

He doesn't say anything.

"Crazy right?"

"Merci, I don't know what to say. My mom hasn't spoken since all of this happened so I had no idea. And with everything going on, I still haven't even been able to bury my dad."

"Shaun, I don't wish what either of our families is going through on anyone. This is a pain that can't be described. However, you have to know that I will stop at nothing to make sure your mom never walks the street again as a free woman."

"I understand and I can't blame you. Please let Pastor and First Lady Alexander know that I am praying for them."

"I will. Thanks for coming."

I leave as he walks into the sanctuary. Getting to the restroom, I splash some cold water on my face hoping it'll take some of the redness from my eyes. I reapply my lip gloss, fix my hair and mentally prepare for the rest of this evening.

Walking back into the sanctuary, I hear loud screaming.

"What is going on here?" I yell above all of them.

"I just came to pay my respects and offer condolences on the passing of Grayce," Warren says.

"You have some nerve showing up here," my dad screams. "Get the hell out of my church, now."

"Melvin, I just wanted to—"

"You wanted to what? See if you can comfort my wife like you did years ago."

"Man, what are you talking about?" Warren asks.

"You know damn well what I mean. Did you come here for Grayce or my wife?"

I step in between them. "Look, I don't know what's going on but this isn't the time or the place. People are starting to arrive and I will not allow either of you to make a mockery of Grayce's memory. Isn't today hard enough without having the both of you in your feelings? Warren, you need to leave."

When he walks out I turn to my dad who throws his hand up and leaves. *SMDH.*

After the many hugs, the multitude of "I'm sorry and you have my condolences," I was glad the visitation was finally over.

Getting to the car, Thomas asks, "What was that about with your dad and that guy?"

"I don't know. This entire family has gotten good at lying so they wouldn't know the truth if it bit them. What I do know is, I don't have the time to deal with it and I won't."

We stop by the hospital to check on Imani before picking up some food and heading home. Thomas's parents are still here and I am glad because, for once, it feels good to be mothered.

"Babe, have you decided what you're going to do with your house?"

"Not yet but most likely I'll sell it. I can't bear the thought of living in it again."

Detective Harris called a few weeks ago to tell me it was released but that house has been the farthest thing from my mind. Thomas has been going by to ensure everything is alright and for now that's enough.

Merci

Making it home, we eat and spend a little time talking to Thomas's parents.

Believe it or not, Thomas and I have yet to consummate our marriage. With all that has been going on, we've never had the time or energy but tonight, I need him.

I take a shower, oil myself all over and wrap a towel around me before walking into the bedroom to find Thomas lying across the bed, on his back, with his eyes closed.

I climb on top of him, startling him. I move up and begin kissing him on the lips.

"I need you," I whisper in his ear.

He doesn't hesitate to respond. He lifts up to remove my towel before his hands roam my body. I moan my pleasure as he rolls me over and is now on top.

He moves in order to take off his pajamas pants before climbing back on top. I wrap my legs around him as he takes one of my breasts in his mouth.

Grabbing the back of his head, I moan. He slowly moves down to my navel, taking his time there before going further to the one place I've been longing for him to touch.

"Hmm," I cry out as he uses his tongue to make my moans louder. "Baby, hmm, please, please; I need to feel you."

He obliges my pleas and wastes no time entering me.

"You feel so good," he whispers in my ear.

I move my hands down to the small of his back as I match his movements. Feeling this man in my arms, inside of me, I release the tears I've held in.

"Babe."

"Please don't stop."

Wrapping my legs tighter, I allow him to make love to my heart and my body. God knows I need it.

"Hmm, yes, oh God."

He grunts as I groan from how good he feels.

I unlock my legs from around him and lift them as I feel my orgasm peaking.

"Oh, right there," I let out as we climax together.

Rising up to look me in the eyes, "I love you Merci Alexander Harvey," he smiles.

"I love you too, baby."

Rolling into his arms, I silently thank God for everything.

Rest well, sister

Pulling up to Memorial Park Cemetery, my stomach fills with butterflies. Grayce requested a graveside service and that's what she's getting.

As I step out the car I smile at the cool breeze blowing, knowing she would have loved this beautiful summer day.

"You ready?"

"No, but I have no choice," I reply, readjusting the black shades on my face.

The funeral directors are there for us to line up. I can already hear my mom sobbing behind me. My dad has been in a somber mood since Grayce died, and since that day at the hospital he has yet to show any bit of emotion.

Grayce's casket is already open at the grave site for a final viewing before the service. Pastor Parker grabs my hand and smiles before he begins reciting scripture and walking toward the grave.

"Do not let your hearts be troubled. You believe in God; believe in Me as well. In My Father's house are many rooms. If it were not so, would I have told you that I am going there to prepare a place for you? And if I go and prepare a place for you, I will come back and welcome you into My presence, so that you also may be where I am. You know the way to the place where I am going.

"The LORD is my shepherd, I lack nothing. He makes me lie down in green pastures, he leads me beside quiet waters, He refreshes my soul. He

guides me along the right paths for his name's sake. Even though I walk through the darkest valley, I will fear no evil, for you are with me; your rod and your staff, they comfort me. You prepare a table before me in the presence of my enemies. You anoint my head with oil; my cup overflows. Surely your goodness and love will follow me all the days of my life, and I will dwell in the house of the LORD forever."

Getting closer to the casket, my legs begin to shake.
"I can't, I can't," I say, turning to walk away. Letting my Mom and Dad go ahead.

"Oh my baby!" Mom screams, causing my dad to finally break. His armor bearer grabs him as he sobs while the funeral home workers support Mom. Dad screams out in a way that signifies his pain.

"The Lord makes no mistakes," he screams. "Lord, God!"

"Baby, you need to see her one last time," Thomas says as his mom and dad surround me.

"I can't. It hurts."

"I know but you need too. Take all the time you need, right now, but you have to see her one last time."

I let out a deep sigh before walking back towards the casket. I bend over into the casket and give her a kiss, "Rest well, baby sister, and I'll see you again somewhere over the rainbow."

As I take my seat, I cannot help but notice two birds playing in the background. Is this a sign from Grayce? I close my eyes and when I reopen them, they are gone. I look around and I don't see them anywhere. *Ok God.*

The mortician begins to close the casket and my dad stops him.

"Wait, please don't close it yet," he says as he stands beside it. Weeping, he begins to say, "I am so sorry Grayce. You didn't deserve to die. You didn't deserve this. Please forgive your daddy."

After kissing her a few times, he is moved only to now have mom back at the casket. She, too, kisses Grayce again before she is removed.

The mortician looks at me and I nod my head for him to close it. I watch as the lid is shut and locked and it's as if peace falls over me. A peace that lets me know she's alright. A peace that calms me knowing she no longer has to deal with this cruel world. A peace that lets me know, although I am sad, she doesn't have to suffer anymore.

This peace gives me comfort.

The service begins and it's a blur as I sit and stare at Grayce's casket the entire time wondering if things could have turned out differently. What if our family had not been so consumed with lies? What if I hadn't left at seventeen? What if I had stood up to my dad? What if I had stayed home? What if—

I am pulled out of my thoughts by Thomas squeezing my hand. I smile at him as Pastor Parker asks for us to place our flowers on her casket.

"In sure and certain hope of the resurrection to eternal life through our Lord Jesus Christ, we commend to Almighty God our sister Grayce and baby Ethan; and we commit their bodies to the ground; earth to earth, ashes to ashes, dust to dust. The Lord bless them and keep them, the Lord make his face to shine upon them and be gracious unto them, the Lord lift up his countenance upon them and give them peace. Amen."

I take my seat again as the services conclude.

"O God, whose mercies cannot be numbered: Accept our prayers on behalf of thy servant Grayce and baby Ethan and grant them an entrance into the land of light and joy, in the fellowship of thy saints; through Jesus Christ thy Son our Lord, who lives and reigns with thee and the Holy Spirit, one God, now and forever. Amen.

"This now concludes the service of our dearly departed, Grayce and Ethan Alexander. We thank you for allowing Harrison Funeral Chapel to handle all of your family needs and we wish you peace and comfort in the days and nights to come. You may now return to your cars."

I don't move as I watch the casket being lowered into the ground.

"Are you sure you want to watch this?" Thomas asks when I don't move.

"Yes. I need to."

"Do you want me to stay?"

"No, go ahead and walk your parents to the car. I'll be on in a minute."

I sit there and watch as they throw dirt on Grayce's casket. They didn't want me to stay but I didn't give them a choice because as I watch them it reminds me that God has me covered. Even through all of this, I am covered by God's grace and mercy. I don't know why this thought comes to me at this particular time but it does and I need it.

I stand, holding another one of the yellow flowers. When I turn Thomas is standing there with his hand out. I smile.

"You okay?" he asks.

"I will be. Thank you, babe."

"You don't ever have to thank me for being by your side."

Repast of lies

The repast is being held at this beautiful place I found not far from the cemetery. I contracted a local catering company to handle the food. Most of the flowers were transported here along with two big, framed pictures of Grayce. I found them on her Facebook page as I read through the many condolences being left there.

She was smiling in them and they captured her true nature and not the girl caught up in the sins of her parents. Even though the media has been running the story of her death as a love triangle gone wrong, it wasn't who she was.

I spent a few hours mingling with church members, friends and folk who just came to be nosey. The crowd is finally dispersing and I've never been so eager to get home but there was something I needed to do first.

"Merci, everything was so beautiful," my mom says walking up to our table.

"Thanks but I can't take all the credit. Grayce left specific instructions. I just made sure they were carried out."

"Well, you handled them well. Didn't she, Melvin?"

"If you say so."

I don't even acknowledge him.

"Are you ready to go?" Thomas asks.

"Not yet," I reply.

"What in the hell is he doing here?" my dad asks staring at the door.

I turn around to see Warren and Marie walking in.

"Melvin, please don't cause a scene," Mom says.

"A scene? Did you invite him?"

"No, I did," I say, turning to greet them. "Warren and Marie, thank you for coming."

"Merci, what is this?" my dad asks.

"It's your day of atonement."

"My day of what?"

"Today is the day you either make amends or the day we sever ties completely," I say to him.

"I don't owe you anything, little girl."

I laugh. "No, you don't, but you'd think losing one daughter would open your eyes to stop you from losing another one but I guess it didn't, huh? You are one cruel, cold son of a bitch. What did I do to you that makes you hate me so much?"

He doesn't answer.

"Tell me!" I scream.

"Look, we only came because Merci asked us," Warren says. "We can see this is a family issue, so we will leave."

"Oh, so now you're worried about my family? Were you worried when you were sleeping with my damn wife?" Dad screams.

Warren looks like he was struck with something.

"What did you say?" I ask. "What does he mean, Warren?"

"I don't know," he says.

I look at my mom and she has her hand to her mouth.

"Go ahead, Warren. Tell everybody how you fucked my wife. Tell them how you made plans to leave your wife for my wife. Oh, and don't forget to tell her how you got my wife pregnant."

"Oh my God!" Mom cries. "Melvin, don't do this."

"I didn't do this, your daughter did."

"Uncle Warren, is this true?" I ask him. "Did you and my mother have an affair?"

He doesn't say anything.

"Answer me, dammit!"

"Yes. We had a brief affair but then she broke it off."

"Is that why you and Daddy stopped being friends?"

"Yes," he says. "I'm sorry. I never meant to hurt any of you. Gina and I were together one night while Melvin was out of town and it—"

"Spare me the details," I say.

"And spare me your apologies," Dad says. "You didn't give a damn about me or your wife, for that matter, because if you did, you never would have been sleeping with my wife."

"It just happened. Marie was never at home and neither were you. You were both traveling a lot with work and Gina and I were lonely and needed companionship."

"No, you were both selfish and only thinking about yourselves," Dad yells.

Marie, Warren's wife, hasn't said anything.

"Marie, did you know about this?" I ask.

"Yes, your father told me."

"Oh, so is that the reason you began sleeping with Dad?"

This time she is the one shocked.

"You didn't think I knew that?" I ask Dad whose eyes are huge.

"You've been sleeping with my wife?" Warren screams, which causes them to all start shouting at each other.

"Shut up!" I scream. "What happened to the baby?"

"What?" Dad asks

"If Mom got pregnant, what happened to the baby?" I ask, looking from my mom to Warren.

"I never knew she was pregnant," he says.

"Mom?"

"I, uh," she stutters. "It's you."

"Me?"

"Yes," she cries. "You're the baby."

"This doesn't make sense. Are you telling me that Warren is my father?"

"Yes."

"But if Warren never knew you were pregnant, then how did Dad find out I wasn't biologically his child?" I ask my mom, who is still crying.

"We all had to take blood tests for some kind of insurance when you were fourteen. When the results came back, it showed you had a different blood type and your dad demanded a DNA test."

"So Merci is *MY* daughter?" Warren asks, looking like he's about to be sick.

"She has to be. You're the only other man I've been with."

"So, Melvin, and I guess I can call you that seeing you're not really my dad. Tell me, is this why you've hated me all this time? The reason you treated me like I wasn't yours?"

"You weren't!" he screamed. "You aren't my daughter!"

"So just so I am clear, I had to pay for Momma's sins yet you forgave her? I had to endure the hate you felt for her yet you slept in the same bed night after night. Is that about right?"

"I don't owe you an explanation."

"Oh, you owe me so much more but I no longer need it or want it. And you got the nerve to call yourself a man of God. You're a joke," I say to him. "And you, Mother, all these years. You allowed him to treat me like I was nothing all so you could live the glamorous life as a pastor's wife. Was it worth it? Was it worth losing both daughters?"

"No! Merci please don't say that. I can't lose you too."

"You lost me the moment you made me pay for what you did. You witnessed how he treated me. You were there the nights he'd call me every name but the one he gave me. You saw, firsthand, his hatred towards me and it was all because you were a hoe. Well, I guess what they say is true. The apple doesn't fall far from the tree."

"What does that mean?" Dad asks.

"Your wife was a whore and so was her daughter Grayce. Wasn't she, Warren?"

"What do you mean?" he asks.

"You were sleeping with Grayce, weren't you?" I smugly ask.

"You what?" Marie screams.

Hearing this, my dad rushes him, throwing a punch that knocks Warren to the ground.

"You sorry motherfucker! You were sleeping with my baby girl. How could you?" Dad yells as he punches him again.

By the time Marie and my mom pull them apart, I have my purse in my hand. "I never want to see any of you again and

I'm glad I got out when I did. An entire family that lies. You all make me sick!"

"Merci, please don't go. I'm sorry," Mom yells after me.

"Yes, you definitely are. You're a sorry excuse for a mother."

Epilogue

3 months later – November

I was finally able to clean out my house before placing it on the market for sale. Going through the desk in my office, I found a note from Grayce that said, *"It is well with my soul. Thank you for everything. You may have been forsaken by Grayce but I was saved by Merci. I love you forever!"* I had it laminated so that I could keep it.

Imani was released from the hospital on September 17, at eight weeks old, with a clean bill of health. She is healthy and strong and the more she grows, the more she resembles Grayce. Oh, the DNA came back negative for Warren being the dad so we suspect it was Darrick although we don't really know for sure.

Regardless, we started the process of adoption while she was in the hospital and it was made official two nights ago. We couldn't be happier. As of November 20, 2016, she is officially Imani Grayce Harvey.

Some nights I stand at her crib and watch her sleep, praying she'll never experience the kind of hurt that has been tied to this family. This is why I pray daily for the generational curses to be broken off our lives. As a parent, I can never see myself inflicting the pain of my sins on her.

As for my parents, my dad has yet to apologize to me but it's not like I was waiting around for it. They are no longer major factors in our lives and the only time we see them is when they come and visit Imani. I decided not to be hateful and keep her from them, no matter how they've treated me. I had to forgive them and I did but that's as far as I am willing to go.

We have a written agreement where they are allowed to get Imani one weekend a month once she turns six months. It was a stretch because I was leaning more towards one weekend a year. *God is working on me.*

Maybe, one day, I'll be able to sit in the same room and hold a conversation but until that day comes, I'll continually pray for them from a distance.

My relationship with Warren is non-existent because his wife, Marie, couldn't bear the thought of him having a child with my mother. I'm good with his decision because, if I'm being honest, I don't see him as father material anyway. Plus, I've spent my life without a dad, so having one now won't change that.

Oh, I do have a relationship with Thomas's parents and it couldn't be more God ordained. They are the best parents any child would be lucky to have and they've been that for me. They don't live far from us so they keep the baby while Thomas and I work.

Speaking of work, with so much going on, the embezzlement case with Mrs. Glassor and Landon was finally resolved. I didn't have to go back to New York because Landon pleaded guilty and received five years in federal prison and ten years' probation. She is required to pay back all of the money she stole, which will probably take her a lifetime.

As for Shaunta Blair, she was declared incompetent to stand trial and was sentenced to life in a mental institution. I was kind of glad because I don't think I could sit through a trial of them explaining how she'd beaten my sister twenty-eight times in the head with a tire iron. When I read the official coroner's report, I knew that God's hand was over Grayce because she shouldn't have survived for as long as she did. Yet, she held on until she made it to the hospital just so Imani would survive. *Isn't God awesome?*

As for her sister who worked in the doctor's office, she was fired. I wanted to press charges on her but in the end, the person responsible for my sister's death is paying for it.

I decided to do an interview with our local news on the effects of domestic abuse. Although Grayce and Darrick weren't married, their affair caused Shaunta Blair to do what she did and, because she was the wife, this was classified as domestic violence.

I didn't do the interview for fame or to even glorify Grayce (she had her part in this too) but I did it because I needed other women and men to see how their actions can have lasting effects on their families. Many don't realize it because it's fun, in the beginning but it doesn't last. Yet the pain does.

Even after everything, Thomas and I have been enjoying being newlyweds. It's hard with a newborn in the house but we find the time. Believe me. It's evident by the fact that we just found out I am pregnant. *Definitely not planned.* We're excited and we have plans to tell his parents over Christmas.

Life has a way of changing and it sometimes happens fast without any input from you. Yet, I take comfort in knowing that God's grace is sufficient for me in my time of weakness.

I visited Grayce's grave for the first time last week, to tell her the latest happenings in my life and I didn't even cry. I looked at her headstone and saw the dash between her birthdate and death date and it made me realize, she'd lived. Although it was short, she still lived. And for that I am grateful.

I wouldn't wish her back here to suffer yet I will live on in her memory because she left a legacy behind and it's in my hands. I have no plans to ruin it.

We all have to die and it makes no sense to live without living! Enjoy every day. And please, stop taking the small things for granted because you'll find yourself missing them when they're gone.

"For our light and momentary troubles are achieving for us an eternal glory that far outweighs them all. So we fix our eyes not on what is seen, but on what is unseen, since what is seen is temporary, but what is unseen is eternal." – 2 Corinthians 4:17-18

Again, I thank you for taking the time to read my work! I cannot express what it means to me every time you support me!

For upcoming contests and give-a-ways, I invite you to like my page, https://www.facebook.com/AuthorLakisha/. Please follow my blog authorlakishajohnson.com or email me at authorlakisha@gmail.com.

If this is your first time reading my work, please check out the many other books available:

- A Secret Worth Keeping, A Secret Worth Keeping: Deleted Scenes and A Secret Worth Keeping 2
- Ms. Nice Nasty, Ms. Nice Nasty: Cam's Confession and Ms. Nice Nasty 2
- Sorority Ties

And my two devotional books:

- Doses of Devotion and You Only Live Once

Also available - Ms. Nice Nasty 2

Camille thought she had the chaos of her life under control until all hell breaks loose. She is brought face to face with Karma and when "they" said Karma's a bitch, they meant it and she is out for Camille's blood. But who is she and why is she hell bent on making Cam suffer?

And it happens to come at a time with the media is digging into her life, putting her career on the line before it can even begin. Then a near fatal accident happens and it wreaks havoc. Along with the sudden death of a friend ... What else can go wrong?

Find out how it all works out for the once Unapologetically Cam!

THANK YOU FOR YOUR SUPPORT!

Made in the USA
Lexington, KY
03 October 2018